OBSIDIOUS

Lucas Pederson

SEVERED PRESS
HOBART TASMANIA

OBSIDIOUS

WWW.SEVEREDPRESS.COM

ISBN: 978-1-925597-16-5

ONE YEAR AGO:
SOMEWHERE IN EASTERN IOWA

In no more than a second, the pale green blip on Private Connor's screen appears, then vanishes. Long enough for him to see it. He frowns, checking the auto-log. Blank. But it shouldn't be. It should show the blip's location and size at the very minimum.

"Somethin' wrong, Connor?" Lieutenant Gibbs bends, her eyes shifting from the screen to him.

Connor shrugs. "There was a blip in sector three, ma'am, but the log didn't record it."

Around them, others are monitoring and analyzing data. Monitor Room Two buzzes and clacks with overly tired enlisted men and women, and grumpy officers. The place smelled like coffee and burnt circuits.

"How long did it last?" Gibbs asks.

"No more than a second, ma'am."

Gibbs nods, straightens. "Sometimes the log misses'em. It's nothing." She begins to turn away, looks at him. "Oh, and Connor?"

He lifts his head to meet her eyes. "Yes, sir?"

"It's ma'am."

Connor watches her walk away, blinks, and turns back to his monitor.

***

A bright flash and she crawls out of the bushes. Her nostrils flare, taking in all the new, strange scents of the life surrounding it.

She doesn't know how she got here, this place with all its green plants, small flying creatures in the trees, and the most unusual ones scuttling on the ground.

She blinks her green eyes, trying to remember what happened before the bright flash and waking up here. One second, she was stalking her prey into a cave, the next…

Three things are perfectly clear, though. This isn't her home. She's cut off from her family. Alone.

She moves forward, blinking, and sets out to do what she has always done.

Survive.

NOW

1

Kris rolls her eyes, picks Tanner's duffel bag up off the cement driveway, and tosses it into the back of the Explorer. Again.

Sometimes, she wishes she was dealing with a lunatic wrapped in explosives rather than her own son.

At least you can shoot the lunatic.

The boy turned sixteen a week ago and already thinks he's king of the castle. Well, she has some shocking news for him today. *She* is king of the goddamn castle.

Kris finds Tanner lounged on the back porch playing on his phone.

"Time to go, bud," she says, keeping her tone neutral.

Tanner smiles at something on his phone, flat out ignoring her.

She blows out a long breath, plucks the phone from his hands.

"Hey! What—?"

Kris cocks a thumb over her shoulder. "Vehicle. Now."

"But I told you I—"

"*Move*."

The boy gives her probably the weakest death glare ever—and she's gotten worse from new recruits—stands, and sulks away.

She pockets the phone, draws in a deep breath, counts to ten, blows it out slowly. Then she returns to the Explorer and hops in.

Tanner sits in his accustomed backseat, arms crossed, glaring straight ahead.

As she puts the Explorer into drive, he says, "Dad wouldn't have made me go."

That stings. Bad. She throws the vehicle into park and turns on him. "Like hell he wouldn't! He loved the outdoors, or don't you remember him anymore?"

Tanner looks away, but she notes the twinkle of tears in his eyes before he does.

Kris sighs. “Look, this’ll be fun. I promise.”

He continues staring out the window, says nothing. Once or twice, he wipes tears from his cheeks. She can yell at him all she wants, but unlike the soldiers she whips into shape, Tanner can’t be broken. Sure, he’s crying. But those aren’t sorry tears, nor wholly sad. They’re angry tears. Pissed off tears.

Kris puts the vehicle in drive and they ride in silence to Brooke’s place.

2

Brooke Sullivan was the Corporal platoon leader in Afghanistan a few years ago, just under Kris in rank.

At first, Kris hated her. Thought her gung-ho attitude would get everyone killed. The woman liked to shoot first and think later. And because they were a reconnaissance team, that was asking for disaster.

Then—after a month or so working together—a bomb collapsed a building they were about to enter. If not for Brooke's quick actions to pull out, they all would've been crushed. After that, Kris didn't hate her so much. But they became friends in a different way.

Not long after the bombing, they were rescuing a couple POWs from a small camp and got stuck under heavy fire. One of the men they saved was really sick and delusional from the tortures he suffered. He scrambled out of their foxhole and Kris went to get him. There was an enemy soldier nearby making a sneak attack. He shot the sick man and pointed his gun at Kris.

Before the bullet left the barrel, Kris was shoved hard to the side. Bam. Bam. Two shots in the dark. Brooke was on the ground where Kris had stood. The enemy soldier dropped to his knees and fell face first in the sand.

Brooke killed him but had also taken the bullet meant for her. Right to the chest.

Once they returned to base camp, Kris stayed with Brooke until the woman woke up. The bullet had missed her heart and anything vital. They've been really close ever since.

Brooke and her son Mark stand in their driveway when Kris rolls up and parks.

When she gets out, Brooke taps her wristwatch. "Always late, lady. *Always*."

Kris shrugs and gives her a hug. When they parted she says, "Ready to go?"

"Pshh, we've been ready for—"

"Ten minutes and sixteen seconds," Mark finishes for her. He grins, pushes his glasses up with an index finger.

Brooke cocks an eyebrow, smiling a bit. "He thinks his super nerd abilities impress me."

Mark smiles. "You made me." Then he loads their bags and tent into the back.

Kris turns to Brooke. "Ethan still being an asshat?"

Brooke snorts and pats Kris's shoulder on the way by. "When isn't he?"

Kris glances at the small, ranch-style house. If Brooke's husband is watching them, he hides well. She restrains herself from flipping off all the windows at once, just in case he's watching. Why Brooke puts up with him is beyond Kris.

"We gonna do this thing, or what?" Brooke calls from the open passenger window of the Explorer.

Kris nods and gets into the vehicle. Brooke rides shotgun.

Tanner had moved to the far back seat, arms crossed, glaring out the tinted window. Mark sits behind Brooke, tapping away at something on his tablet.

"Mel flake out yet?" Brooke asks as Kris puts the Explorer into reverse.

"Not yet," Kris says. "But it's about five minutes to her place, so…"

"Yup," Brooke says. "I give it two minutes before you get a text."

Kris rolls out of Brooke's driveway.

3

One wouldn't think the small Hispanic woman standing outside the red-brick apartment building was a captain in the United States Army.

Nothing about her reveals a command presence. From her gray and brown hiking shoes to the checkered green flannel shirt, one might either think she's gone fruitbatty up in the ol' noggin, or homeless.

Neither is the case. To be honest, Melanie Hernandez acts and dresses this way on purpose. Because in the Army, she is tough, rigid, and sometimes cold, she counters all of that with goofiness and frumpy warmth while away. She doesn't like hunting, nor camping.

She confessed to Kris the other day that it all reminded her of the Army, even it was just for fun, just to get out and enjoy nature and their kids.

The guns. The woods. The tents. To her, it's like they were out on their next mission to rescue more POWs.

Standing next to Mel is her daughter, Avery, not looking as outdoorsy as her mom in black boots, black jeans, and a camo jacket. She completes the ensemble with fingerless, black gloves.

Kris gets out of the Explorer. "Hey! You two ready?"

Mel rolls her eyes toward her daughter who nods, eyes wide. All smiles. Totally excited. Mel looks at Kris. "Well, of course *she* is."

Kris helps them place their stuff in the back and closes the hatch.

"You know," Kris says to Mel before the woman crams in with the two teenagers in back, "this'll be fun if you let it."

Mel snorts in her best sarcastic way. Which isn't very good. "We'll see."

Kris shuts the door once Mel squeezes in. Then she glances at the apartment building where Mel lives.

The woman never married and Avery was the result of a one-night stand during Mel's "party period." She didn't even know the guy's name. And even though Kris and Brooke have tried setting her up with great guys, she never followed through. Eventually, they just gave up on Mel and let her be who she wanted to be. It all worked out okay, anyway.

Kris met Mel shortly after Brooke. Mel was assigned to their platoon, and they all hit it off once Kris and Brooke figured the woman out.

She climbs into the Explorer, and they begin the two-hour drive to Maker's Woods up north.

4

An hour or so later, Tanner pipes up, “Hey! I gotta pee, Mom!”

Brooke chuckles. “Is he always that demanding?”

Kris sighs. “Only when he wants to be a pain in my ass.”

“Must be a teen thing.” Brooke grins.

“Or just a Tanner thing,” Kris says.

“Nah. Mark can be—”

“I can hear you,” Mark says.

Brooke half turns in her seat. “You know, children are supposed to be seen and not heard, right?”

Kris can almost see the eye roll when Mark says, “Pshh, yeah, maybe in the 1930s.”

Brooke looks at Kris. “See? Thinks he’s Mr. Know it All.”

Mel says, “You should see the things he’s doing on that tablet, though…”

Brooke sighs. “Better not be porn again.”

Mel chuckles. “No. Looks like some kind of coding app or—”

“Old people,” Mark says. “I’m trying to design a game here. Shh.”

Tanner mumbles something from the far back, but Kris can’t make out the words. Probably nothing nice, though. The boy is being an ass, like usual.

Avery scoots closer to Mark. “What kind of game?”

“Just a shooter,” Mark says. “I—”

“Mom,” Tanner shouts. “Do you want me to pee all over back here?”

Kris loves the kid. Very much. But with days like this, it takes every last bit of her strength not to strangle him. She takes the first off ramp and parks at a convenience store.

“Thank God.” Tanner thumps the back of Mel’s seat. “Hurry.”

Kris notes the stony expression on Mel’s face, the one she normally reserves for work or on a mission. But instead of unloading a barrage of anger, she opens the door and lets Tanner out. The boy at least thanks her. That’s good. Progress.

“Anyone else gotta go?” Kris asks, getting out to stretch her legs a bit.

Brooke and Mel join her as Mark and Avery chat about Mark’s game-making skills. To Kris, Mark looks like he’s in heaven having Avery so close.

As if to shine a light on this, Brooke nudged Mel and says, “I think your kid has a crush on my kid.”

Mel pshhed. “Other way around, woman.”

They all chuckle as the warm, midmorning September sun caresses their skin. Soon, Kris knows, fall will really set in, ushering out the warmth for the bitter icy teeth of winter. But right now, the weather is still warm. Not too hot. Not too chilly. Perfect camping weather. The kind where a fire is amazing during the day, but needed at night if one wanted to roast marshmallows, or whatever.

Tanner hops into the back and they all climb into the Explorer to finish the drive.

Kris smiles. Despite Tanner’s attitude, the trip should be a blast. Once he realizes how fun it’ll be, she’s sure he’ll come around.

She hopes so, anyway.

5

"Wait, what?" Tanner asks, glances up the rutted dirt road into the woods.

"It won't kill ya." Kris slings the strap of her duffel bag over her shoulder. "Now grab your bag and the tent, please."

He blinks at her like she just spoke to him in some alien language. "Why do I have to carry the tent?"

"Dude," Mark says, walking by carrying a tent. "Stop being a douche."

"Shut your fat face-hole, man," Tanner says.

"Tanner!" Kris about slaps him. "Apologize! Now!"

The boy grumbles something, picks up the tent, and says, "Sorry," to Mark.

Mark shrugs and continues on, following behind Mel, Brooke, and Avery.

Once they're out of earshot, Kris turns on her son. "What the hell is your deal? I know you didn't want to come here, but treating other people like that isn't who you are."

Tanner sighs. "I dunno. Just...yeah, I'm sorry. I miss Dad, okay?"

That softens her a bit. "I do, too. So much. But you know, I really think he would've wanted you to have fun out here. He loved the outdoors. Hunting especially."

"I know," Tanner says and walks away.

Kris grabs the bag of ammo and their rifles, wishing Kyle was there.

Kyle always knew what to do with Tanner. But her husband had been dead for a year. A Marine killed by a drunk driver. A hero taken down by not a bullet, but a man named Bill Randle who was finishing up his fifth of vodka as he plowed the snow-laden streets. Kyle was two blocks from home when Bill swerved into his lane, crushing their car and Kyle along with it.

Two blocks. Another three minutes or so, and Kyle would've been pulling into the driveway. Safe. Still alive.

Kris thinks about him every day. Thinks about that night and how drastically life can change in a blink.

Three minutes and he would've been home…

She huffs out a breath, makes sure her tears are in check, and follows the others into Maker's Woods.

SOMEWHERE IN EASTERN IOWA

General Berk hates mornings. Always has. And the loathing is just getting worse as he grows older.

Only two more years, he reminds himself every morning. *Two more years and I can retire and sleep in as late as damn well want to.*

He's just easing himself into the cushy chair behind his desk when Private Silva knocks on his doorjamb.

Berk almost draws his Smith and Wesson pistol and shoots the boy. Instead, he says, "Yes, Private?"

Silva snaps a salute and says, "Sorry to bother you so early, sir, but there are some thermal images that I've just become aware of you might want to see."

Berk sighs, sips on his coffee, and motions to Silva. "Send 'em to my computer, Private Silva. I'll take a look after I get some of this paperwork crap out of the way."

Silva doesn't move.

One verge of irritation, Berk barks, "What?"

"Sir, the images."

"Come on, Private. I don't have all damn day. Spit it out."

"Sir, the images…they're not human."

Berk frowns.

And so begins the longest day of his life.

6

Not many people camp this deep into Maker's Woods nowadays. Gone is the golden age of roughing it in the wild for a weekend. Everyone prefers their campers, flushing toilets, and electricity too much.

Which is sad because, as they hike up the final hill where the dirt road ended, Kris finds herself completely taken by nature. With the leaves already turning their vibrant fall colors and the weeds beginning to brown and curl. With the birdsongs filling the dry, slightly cooler air under the tree canopy. The sweet smells of life. All of it. It's beautiful.

"Hey, boss," Brooke shouts from the dead end of the road to Kris. "Um, where we going?"

They've been camping in Maker's Woods before, just not so deep in. Kris figures it'll give them all a sense of adventure to find their own special campsite this time.

She waves them all forward, walking toward Brooke. "Keep going. Let's see if we can find a nice clearing."

"You mean you don't even have a spot picked out?" Mel asks, but she's smiling a little, obviously enjoying it all now.

"Nope," Kris says and plunges through the screen of brush into the woods.

A moment later, she hears them following behind her. She kicks her way through thorny brambles and makes a rudimentary path for them. Sticks snap dryly like cap guns under her boots as she trudges onward.

Yes. This is going to be great.

7

Kris places the guns and ammo on the ground and turns to the others.

"It'll need new drapes but…" Brooke kicks the dead tree dividing the clearing. "It'll do. I guess." Then she sticks her tongue out at Kris.

Kris returns the gesture.

"So where do we set up?" Mel asks.

Kris shrugs. "Anywhere."

Brooke nudges Mark. "Make sure they get the spot with the anthill."

Mark grins and begins setting up their tent. Mel and Avery step over the dead tree and set up on the other side.

"So," Kris says to Tanner. "Where should we sleep?"

Tanner glances at the others, then looks at her. "Right here?"

Kris smiles. "If we do, Brooke gets her wish."

He gives her a WTF look.

She lowers her gaze to the ground in front of him. He follows the gaze and stumbles backward.

Kris chuckles as Tanner frantically brushes ants off his boots and jeans. His face has a pinched, angry glare fixed to it. Even so, he's laughing while he brushes the last of the ants off of himself. She almost tells him that at least it isn't fire ants, then thought better of it… Because they're fire ants.

They end up pitching the tent beside Brooke and Mark.

It doesn't take long to make the small clearing their own. Mel burns out the anthill, digs it up, and makes it into a fire pit. Soon, she has a nice, roaring inferno going, with flames as tall as Kris and four feet wide. No one can stand within five feet of it. Too damn hot.

Mel says, "Gotta make it big if we're going to cook our own meat." She tosses in a length of wood from the dead tree. Sparks spiral up out of the flames.

"Do you want to start a forest fire?" Brooke says. "Because this is how you start forest fires."

Mel humphs. "The average doe weighs between ninety and two hundred pounds." They all kind of blink at her. She smiles. "Not that we'll be hunting deer."

"What *are* we hunting?" Avery asks.

"Turkey," Kris replies.

"Um…" Mark says. "Turkey season doesn't start until October."

"Thank you, prodigy boy," Tanner whispers.

Mark rolls his eyes.

"Yep," Kris says. "We're early. But I talked to the DNR before making plans. They agreed to just one turkey each. No more."

"Well then," Brooke says. "Why are we still here worshiping the Queen of Fire over there and not bagging us some turkeys?"

Kris gestures toward the woods beyond their clearing. "Ready when you are."

"What?" Tanner says. "Now?"

"Probably won't hunt today, but we need to set up some blinds," Kris says.

"Blinds?"

She keeps forgetting this is Tanner's first hunting trip.

"Branches and stuff to hide us from the turkeys," she says, smiling.

"Oh."

They find a nice hollow not far from camp and set up their blinds up wind along the edge.

Kris tells Tanner, "So when the turkeys go down there, they'll be easy pickings. Always good to have the high ground."

"Sir, yes, sir," Tanner says.

She claps his shoulder. "It's *ma'am*, smartass."

Tanner laughs and she laughs with him. He's coming around. And by the time the weekend is over, he'll want to do it again. Sometimes, you have to just drag someone out of their norm and make them experience things.

They're all walking back to camp, dead leaves crunching under their boots, when Avery stops and points at an old oak tree.

"Hey, look," she says.

They gather around the tree.

"Bear, you think?" Mel asks.

Kris shook her head. "There aren't any bears in Iowa."

"Um," Mark says. "Black bears sometimes wander this far south from Minnesota, though."

After another moment, Brooke says, "Well, everyone stay close to camp." She gives the kids each a stern look. "Don't go off by yourself. And we'll have to keep our food sealed up tight."

Kris hangs back while the others make their way back to camp. She stares at the tree. She isn't so sure about the bear theory. It's possible, she supposes. But…

She runs her fingertips along the ragged claw marks cut into the tree. All the way through the tough bark to the white meat of the trunk. Black bear claws can't do that, can they?

Kris cranes her neck, inspecting the tree. The claw marks go all the way up.

"You get lost?" Mel asks, startling Kris a bit. When Mel notices, she adds, "Are you okay? Not like you to be so jumpy."

Kris bites her bottom lip. She says, "Yeah, I'm fine." She drapes an arm over Mel's shoulders. "We better feed them before they go feral."

They chit-chat the rest of the way to camp.

Behind them, a few dead leaves see-saw to the ground.

8

It takes Kris ten minutes to wake Tanner up. Even then the boy shoos her away.

It's 7:00 in the morning.

"Come on, kid," she says. "Let's bag us a turkey."

"I don't even like turkey on Thanksgiving, though."

"Yes, you do," Kris says. "Trust me, I've watched you pig out on it. Now get up and get dressed."

Tanner tosses the sleeping bag off with a gruff sigh and gets dressed.

By the time Kris and Tanner emerge from their tent, the others are already around the fire drinking coffee.

Brooke snorts. "Well, there ya are, sleepyheads."

Kris drinks some coffee, because she needs it to keep from killing Tanner if he decides to be an ass later, but also to warm her up a bit. The morning has an icy bite to it, a prelude to the bitter winter yet to come.

Her late husband, Kyle, used to love winter. Loved the snow, cold, all of it. In fact, he'd been on his way back home from a skiing trip with a couple of his buddies the night the drunk plow driver Bill crushed him to death. So, in a way, it was almost like the winter he loved had killed him.

On the other hand, she hates winter. All of it. The cold most of all. But she hates it even more so after what she's coming to think of as the worst night of her life: Kyle's death.

After a couple cups of Mel's strong brew, Kris readies her rifle and Tanner's twelve-gauge shotgun. The shotgun is pump action; easy to use and will fire five shells before needing to reload.

Since Tanner was ten, either she or Kyle had taken the boy out target practicing, taught him gun safety and all of the fundamentals.

So he knows very well how to handle a gun. Even side arms. In fact, she bought a Colt .45 for his sixteenth birthday, planning on giving it to him after he shoots his first turkey this weekend. And even if he doesn't make his first kill, she'll give it to him anyway.

It's what Kyle would have wanted; what they'd agreed on before he died.

The boy sits by himself on a portion of the fallen tree. He stares off either into the woods, or into nothing at all. He wears the new camo jacket she bought especially for this weekend. The expression on his face is one of the deepest boredom. Or maybe he's getting into the zone, focusing himself for the hunt.

Ha. Yeah, sure. And pigs are unicorns. No, more than likely he's bored. Probably misses his phone (which was left back in the Explorer) and all the eases and luxuries of the modern world. He has friends, but rarely actually hangs out with them nowadays. They text and message and video chat, but gone are the days of hogging out on pizza and playing video games. Gone are the days of grabbing their fishing poles and heading out to Miller's Pond to catch bass, or sunfish, or nothing at all.

Days when they were really friends.

Kris sits beside him, sighs. "We're about ready, kid."

Tanner nods. Says nothing.

"Penny for your thoughts?"

Now he looks at her. "Huh?"

She smiles. "What are ya thinking about?"

"Oh," he says. "Um, nothing much. Just trying to enjoy this nature thing, I guess."

"Your dad loved nature. Do you remember?"

Tanner stares into the line of trees ahead. "Yeah."

"You two gonna talk all day," Brooke calls, "or are we gonna shoot us some turkeys?"

Kris says, "Go ahead. We'll be right behind you."

Brooke glances at Mel. Mel chuckles a bit and leads them out of the clearing. Kris turns back to Tanner.

"Mom," he says. "Really. I'm okay."

"I just want you to have fun out here," she says. "You don't look like you're having fun."

He laughs a little under his breath. “Yeah.” Then he stands, picks up his shotgun, and follows the others, leaving Kris to stare after him.

9

Kris nudges Tanner, waking him from a light doze.

If he'd been a private, she would've battered him with a barrage of shouts about disrespect and made him run until he puked.

But he's her son. And a teenager.

His mouth moves. She presses a finger to his lips. She points into the hollow where an entire family of turkeys pecks at the ground. They make gobbling sounds like turkeys do. There's a tom, big and puffy, strutting around, and three females. If done right, they might all get their turkeys for the weekend this morning. Which will be awesome. Then tomorrow they can just relax.

She gives Brooke and Mel the signal to fire at the same time and be ready. They both nod and instruct their kids on what to do. Kris watches Mark and Avery aim their shotguns and then she turns to Tanner. He blinks at her like he never even considered shooting a real turkey before.

Kris points at the turkeys, nods. *Shoot one*, she tries to convey. Still, he blinks at her like she's dumb. She gently grabs the barrel of his gun and points the muzzle through the hole in the blind. She nods at him again.

Tanner's lips press together, forming a pale line across his bronzed face. It isn't an expression of defiance, but one of focus. Of someone knowing what needs to be done, and not really liking the idea much.

A turkey will mark his first kill.

When the boy was eight, he asked Kyle why people liked to hunt animals. It was a Saturday evening, right after supper, and they were getting ready to watch a movie together. Kyle just smiled and said, "People hunt for different reasons, bud."

Tanner frowned, but nodded like he understood, then asked, "Why do *you* hunt, Dad?"

Kyle chuckled and said, "I have a few reasons of my own."

"Like?"

"We're just full of questions tonight, aren't we?" Kyle chuckled.

Tanner grinned, shrugged.

Kyle reached over and ruffled Tanner's hair. "It's okay. No, my number one reason is to be out there. To be in nature. It doesn't even matter if I shoot a deer or turkey. Usually just being out there is enough."

"You like the woods?" Tanner kind of sneered at the idea.

"Oh, yes. Love it. The sounds, smells…all of it." Kyle paused and gave Kris the thumbs up for a movie she picked out. "But," he continued. "I also hunt for the meat. For food."

Tanner made a face. "Food? Ew!"

Kyle's eyes hardened a little. "Not ew. It's the purest meat."

They were quiet for a moment, then Kyle sighed. His hard gaze softened. "What do you think the hamburgers were made of we ate tonight, bud?"

"Uh, cow?"

"Nope." Kyle shook his head slowly. "That was venison."

"Veni-*huh*?"

"Venison. Deer meat."

The expression of shock that stole over Tanner's face was both comical and beautiful. Then he smiled.

"I liked it," he said and cuddled closer to Kyle as Kris started the movie. She sat next to her boys, sandwiching Tanner in.

Now, Tanner aims the shotgun at one of the turkeys. Kris isn't sure which one, but assumes the tom. Hell, they're probably all aiming for the tom. He's the biggest, after all. No one wants the smaller females. Not as showy and meaty as the tom.

Kris holds a fist up to Mel and Brooke. They whisper to Mark and Avery.

In Tanner's ear, she says, "When I touch your shoulder, you can shoot your turkey."

He nods, focused.

It has to be this way. All three shooting at once, otherwise one missed shot might result in the turkeys running out of the hollow.

She smiles. He hasn't focused on anything like this besides his phone for the last year or so.

She holds a fist up again and—

Dead leaves explode upward in a geyser of color. The turkeys shriek. Something moves fast through the falling leaves, a blur Kris can't get a fix on, like it blends in with everything. Only movement gives it away.

BOOM. Tanner fires his shotgun. A shrill scream cuts through the shrieking turkeys. Kris's heart quakes. A chill shivers through her. Her breath snags in her throat like a rusty fishhook.

A mixture of leaves and feathers flutter to the ground. Kris blinks, shakes her head, and looks again. The turkeys are gone. All of them.

"What…?" Tanner, his voice barely above a whisper.

Kris glances at Brooke and Mel. They look back at her, appearing just as bewildered. Mel rolls a shoulder in a shrug. The woods go utterly silent around them. Not a bird sings, nor a cricket chirp. Kris stands, eyes scanning the trees and brush around the hollow. Her grip tightens on the rifle in her hands.

"What the hell *was* that?" Brooke asks, stepping beside Kris.

Kris focuses on the turkey feathers for a moment, then says, "Not a bear."

"We should go down there," Mel says. "See if there are tracks. Maybe it's a mountain lion."

Brooke snorts. "Yeah, one on speed. I mean, did either of you actually *see* it?"

Kris shakes her head.

"No," Mel says. "Just a blur."

"Kids," Kris says. "Stay here. We're gonna go take a look."

"What was it?" Mark asks. "All I saw were leaves."

"Same," Avery spouts. "Maybe it's like an escaped panther?"

"An escaped *panther*?" Mark sniggers. "Escaped from where? I don't think…"

The rest Kris tunes out as all three women make their way down the gradual slope into the hollow. They still hold their rifles tight, still locked and loaded. Dead leaves crackle under their boots.

"I've never seen anything move so fast." Mel crouches down, inspecting the scatter of brown, black, and white feathers.

"I don't even think a panther moves that fast." Brooke frowns at something not far from the feathers.

"They don't," Kris says, staring at the leaves.

Not all of the turkeys were taken. Lying partially hidden in leaves, she spies a beak. She toes it with her boot and the tom's severed head rolls out of the leaves. Now she notices other things. Tidbits here and there like grotesque Cracker-Jack prizes. Claw-feet. An eyeball rests on a curled oak leaf. Sprinkles of blood.

"Hey," Brooke says. She's crouched in the spot she'd been staring at a few seconds before, a few feet from the feather and nasty tidbits of turkey. "You gotta see this."

Kris and Mel glance at each other. Mel's eyes are the stony gray she typically reserves for work. Kris doesn't care for the change. It somehow solidifies that something bad really did happen. As though she doesn't already know it's bad, Mel's hard eyes confirm it.

They walk over. Brooke pushes a slimy, black substance around with a small stick. Small globs on a few dead leaves.

"Yep," Kris says after a moment. "That's weird. But what—?"

"Watch," Brooke says.

She stabs the end of the stick into one of the larger globs. The black stuff leeches onto the stick and climbs up. It crawls to about an inch away from Brooke's fingers. She tosses the stick away, visibly shivers.

As Kris watches, the black stuff coils around the stick and—

Crack. It snaps in two.

"Jesus," Mel says, her voice breathy. "Did it really just *do* that?"

"Uh, yeah," Brooke says. She stands and turns to Kris and Mel. "I think that stuff is that thing's blood. Whatever *it* is."

"Shit," Kris says. Her heart knocks too fast. She draws in slow breaths trying to calm it. Doesn't work.

"Tanner fired his gun," Brooke says. "Maybe he wounded it."

"But what the hell *is* it?" Mel says, voice very low.

Both Kris and Brooke shake their heads.

Kris's gaze drifts to the blind where Tanner watches her. "It's like it can blend in with things. Like wearing better camo than the military can ever dream up."

"No one dreams up better camo than us, though," Mel says.

"Someone did, I think," Kris says.

"You guys talk like it's a person that did this," Brooke blurts. "Didn't you see how fast it was? Nothing moves like that in nature. Not even a damn cheetah."

Kris sighs, blinks. On the far side of the hollow stands a large, ancient pine tree. A big white pine, she guesses. It goes up so high she has to strain her neck to see the top. But it isn't its age that catches her eye, nor its height.

About six or seven feet up the trunk are deep gouges in the bark. All the way to white meat of the tree.

Claw marks.

"Whatever it is," she says, "it's probably leaving those marks, too."

"Boss," Brooke says. "Maybe we better pack it up and go home. I'm getting a bad vibe about this place."

Kris lowers her head, feeling the same exact bad vibe. Brooke is right. Maybe they better get out. It's apparent something strange is in the woods. But…

She looks at Mel and Brooke. "It hasn't attacked us. And besides, we're trained soldiers. Special Recon soldiers. We know our shit. We'll take turns on watch detail tonight and—"

"Are you serious?" Brooke shoots a glance up the slope of the hollow to the kids, then fixes her sight on Kris. "I'm not going on watch detail when I don't have to." Her voice lowers. "There's something bad in these woods with us."

"This isn't for us," Kris says. "It's for them." She gestured at the kids.

Brooke spins away, grumbling something under her breath.

Mel says, "Okay. We'll take shifts watching. But I agree with Brooke, too. We *should* leave."

"You guys don't get it," Kris says. "*Kyle* planned this for Tanner's sixteenth birthday. This is *his* idea. I can't just pack up and leave without honoring that much of him."

"Oh, no." Mel steps closer to Kris. "I get it. Absolutely. But if that thing is dangerous, you're putting our kids in danger. Not just us."

Kris flaps her arms up in exasperation. "If it wanted to get us, it would've already. But if you two wanna go, then go. I'm not stopping you."

"What, and walk all the way home?" Brooke's cheeks flush a deep scarlet. "Unless you hand over your keys."

"Fine." Kris pulls the Explorer keys from her pocket and tosses them to Brooke.

Brooke catches them and rolled her eyes. "We're a team." She lobs the keys back. "And we'll stay. I'm just more than a little freaked out, you know?"

Pocketing the keys, Kris says, "Yeah. Me, too. But maybe it's nothing. Maybe we blinked at the wrong moment, making it seem like it was faster than it really was."

Brooke lifts an eyebrow. "Did we all blink at the same time?"

Kris shrugs. "Maybe?"

Mel steps in between them. Their captain. "Both of you…stand down. This is what we're going to do. We watch in shifts. Just like we're in the field. But, Brooke, I also agree with Kris. It hasn't done anything to us beside spook us a little. Could be just a wolf that came down from the north. They do that too, like bears. But fighting over it solves nothing. Or did you forget your training?"

Kris releases a long breath she hadn't known she'd been holding. It's like boot camp all over again. The feelings and uncertainties, anyway. Not so much the physicality. Still, Mel puts on her captain's hard hat.

They need it.

Sometimes, they all need to be put in check from time to time. Or at least reminded of who they are and what they do.

Brooke smiles wearily. "Sorry, Boss."

Kris smiles back. "Happens."

A long moment of silence drapes between all three of them then. Long enough for Kris to reconsider Brooke's edginess to get the hell out of Maker's Woods, however brief.

Then Mel, walking away, says, "You two start crying in each other's arms, I'll steal the keys and leave *both* your sorry butts here."

They laugh, but Kris knows the woman isn't joking. She'll sure as shit leave them here. Mel doesn't care for the whole stereotypical sisterly things. Like crying into each other's arms, or shopping, or drama. Kris feels the same. Nothing about them is stereotypical, and changing that now, even in thought, will be damaging to their friendship.

Later, with the blinds moved to the edge of a meadow—well, more like another clearing, but meadow somehow sounds more adventurous—away from the hollow, they wait for more turkeys to come along. Kris sits with Tanner, watching, but not watching the clearing, her mind still trying to wrap itself around what happened in the hollow.

Could it really be a panther or something? She lets this question linger in the forefront of her mind for a moment before dismissing it entirely. Brooke is absolutely right. Nothing natural can move so fast, let alone snatch up four big turkeys in one swoop. So, the bigger question is: What took the turkeys?

A question, she feels, will never be answered.

10

Kris checks her wristwatch, and it's about six o'clock in the afternoon. She waits another ten minutes. The clearing remains deserted, save for the sparse weeds and a scattering of redwing blackbirds. Then she tells Tanner to pack it up for the day.

"Lame," he says, stands.

"Yeah," she says. "Sorry, kid. Maybe tomorrow."

Tanner favors her with a ghost of a smile. "Yeah. Okay. Will some weird thing steal our turkeys again?"

Kris lowers her head a bit, not sure what to say to this.

He stretches. "So what's for supper? Tree bark and berry stew?"

She grins. "If that's what you wanna eat, but I think we're having open-fire burgers or something mundane like that."

It's the first time since the trip she hears Tanner truly laugh. The best sound in the world, and oh how she's missed it.

They make the long trek back to camp, no one talking. Kris, Brooke, and Mel remain alert. Eyes always moving through the woods, picking out potential enemies as they're trained to do. Kris only encounters a few more claw marks on the trees. That's all. If it's stalking them, she doesn't see, nor hear any signs. Neither do Mel and Brooke, apparently.

Good, Kris thinks. *Maybe that means the thing is long gone.* And on top of this, *maybe we should pack up and leave*. She is still teetering on the idea.

If not for Kyle, she probably would've gotten them all out after the hollow incident.

But this trip is for Kyle as well as Tanner; a memorial of sorts to honor the man she still loves… And a way to show her son how much she loves him. Her boys.

Brooke calls back, "Hey, Boss, you're our cook this evening. Mel said so!"

"Court-martial," Mel says in a dry tone.

They all laugh at that. Even the kids.

The day might have been a waste and a totally bizarre one, but the hunting part isn't the sole reason for the trip anyway. The main reason is to get out and away from the world for a couple days. Together. The reason is to have fun. And right now, this very moment, that's all that matters.

11

Brooke brought along a tripod with a cast-iron grill, which attaches to the top of the contraption with a chain. It hangs over the fire to pretty much cook everything. She sets the thing up while Kris forms and seasons the burgers.

Mel sits with Mark, Avery, and Tanner, telling true-life war stories. Tanner seems to even be enjoying himself for once. Kris smiles, watching him as she prepares the burgers and is struck, smack in the face, with a simple fact she typically tries to ignore.

Tanner is growing up. Gone is the round-faced boy who clung to her leg when friends came to visit. Gone is the baby she rocked and sang to sleep at night. Gone is the boy who would crawl into her bed when a thunderstorm crashed outside.

Tanner grew up on her. Overnight, too, it seems.

Kyle would be a proud dad right now, though.

As she watches, she also notices how angular his face appears. So much like his father. The chubby cheeks are but a distant memory. Her heart aches and rejoices at the same time. Loss and gain swing hand in hand.

She cooks the burgers.

As they finish their meal, birds sing their final goodbyes to the light as the crickets and frogs usher in the night. What Kris hates most about this time of year are the shorter days. It gets dark around eight o'clock, rather than nine or ten.

Sitting on fold-up canvas chairs around the fire, stomachs full, they chit-chat about various topics. Mark and Avery, growing closer and closer since yesterday, are pretty much inseparable. And although Kris doubted Mark notices at all, Avery hung on his every word. He is always so absorbed in his gaming codes and idea for new games, he rarely acknowledges she's practically batting her eyes at him.

Boys…

Tanner seems to have found a kindred spirit in Brooke, though. Currently, they're discussing how dumb the recent presidential candidates are. Huh, first time for everything, she supposes.

Mel leans back in her chair and smiles at all the stars winking through the opening in the tree canopy. "You know, this is pretty nice. Just relax and soak it all in."

"You must've eaten Brooke's 'special' brownies again," Kris says, grins.

Mel snorts. "A girl makes one mistake and she never lives it down." She looked at Kris. "My friends are assholes, apparently."

In front of them, the fire crackles and pops. Flames lick the night air in reds, oranges, yellow, and streaks of blue.

Mel found a dead red cedar tree not far from camp earlier and tossed in a few chunks after supper.

The aroma is divine. Fresh cedar smells great, but burning cedar…there are no other smells that really compare. Like the inside of cigar humidor, perhaps, but not quite.

Kris looks away from the fire. "Brooke was right."

"Of course she was," Mel says and gulps down some soda. She burps and adds, "but so are you. Thought one of you was going to drop down and start bawling on me."

"Yeah," Kris says. "Look at us. All girly and stuff."

"Disgusting," Mel says and downs the rest of her soda.

They chat into the night, and when bedtime comes, Kris takes the first watch.

12

The fire dies to glowing coals. She tosses another chunk of wood in. Not cedar, but some other type of wood she doesn't recognize. The flames brighten the entire clearing for a few minutes. She adds three more heavy chunks and sits down, rifle across her lap.

The crickets and frogs share their nightly orchestra with her.

After a moment, she stands and walks the perimeter of the camp, eyes and ears focusing on the darkness beyond the firelight. Other than the crickets and frogs, the woods lay silent, sleeping.

Kris zips her jacket up. Getting chilly now. Not cold, but somewhere in between miserable and tolerable. The gray area of temperatures.

She checks her watch and sits back down.

Three more hours and she'll have to wake Mel up.

But, as happens during watches, boredom settles in and takes up residence.

Kris sighs. Someone in one of the tents is snoring. She smiles, suspecting Brooke. The woman always snores. It's one of the reasons why they need an inside place to sleep in the field or she'll give away their location.

But this isn't war. They aren't on a mission. They are like sisters. Brooke, Mel, and her. They argue and bicker. Love and laugh. They care about each other at work and at home.

She leans her rifle against the side of the chair and stirs the coals with a thick stick Brooke used a few hours before. Soon, she'll have to add more wood to keep the fire alive and bright.

Another hour slogs by and she finds herself nodding off in the chair. She sits up straight, shakes her head, lightly slaps her cheeks. When none of this works, she stands and places more chunks of wood onto the coals. If they want breakfast in the morning, someone will have to chop more from the fallen tree cutting their camp in half.

She gulps down a soda, hoping the caffeine and sugar will at least give her a good enough buzz to coast her through the remaining hour.

Twenty minutes later, chin sinking to her chest, she drifts off into a deep sleep as the fire slowly dies.

Another handful of minutes later, the crickets and frogs cease their serenade, and silence creeps in.

***

Avery has to pee.

She crawls out of the tent, zips it up, and glances at Kris snoozing in the chair in front of the fire.

She smiles and turns to a cluster of bushes not far from their tent.

Her bladder sloshes with every step. Her face twists in concentration. The last thing she wants is to pee her pants, especially if Mom finds out and lets it slip tomorrow. Then Mark will know and, well…ugh. She doesn't want to deal with that. Not at all.

She pee-dances her way to the bushes.

Avery steps into the bushes. They rustle for a second or two, then fall still.

She never comes back out.

13

She stands in a dark tunnel and someone is screaming. It echoes off the walls, but distant, like someone shouting from the other end of a football field.

Still, she walks toward the screaming. Curious. Because, really, who would be screaming down a tunnel? Doesn't make any sense. She wants to help whoever it is, though. She *needs* to help. So her walk turns into a run. And the closer she gets, the louder the screaming, and—

Kris jerks awake, and the screaming follows. Not so distant now.

Mingling in the scream are people shouting a name over and over. She sits there, staring at the smoldering ashes. Smelling the char of the wood. Birds singing. It's morning.

Then it all snaps together in her head. She sucks in a slow breath, eyes widening.

"Avery," Brooke shouts.

"AAAVEEERY!" That's Mark.

"AAVERY!" Tanner.

And—

"You bitch."

Kris turns her head. The punch knocks her out of the chair. A brilliant pain ignites through her head. For a few seconds, she has no clue who she is. The punch is *that* hard. *That* unexpected.

The pain turns into a horrid ache just below her right eye. Feels like her eyeball is about to pop right out its damn socket. Her entire head throbs, on the verge of exploding. At least that's what it feels like, anyway.

Mel stands over her, hands balled into tight, shaking fists. Her eyes… Kris knows those eyes. They're stonier than ever now, though. Hard. Cold. Somewhere in the region between rage and sorrow.

"You," Mel says.

"Me?" Kris sits up, tentatively touches her cheekbone with the tips of her fingers. The pain is immediate and raw. She sucks in a sharp breath through clenched teeth.

"You were supposed to wake me up," Mel cries. She kicks dirt and leaves at Kris. "You were supposed to be watching! Now she's…she's…" Mel, tears trickling down her cheeks, spins away.

Brooke helps Kris to her feet.

"I—what happened?"

Brooke looks at her with bloodshot eyes; her face haggard, almost old. "Avery is missing."

"*What*?" Kris's eyes dart, heart tripping over itself. She starts toward the woods.

Brooke grabs her. "We need to stay together. We're a team, remember?"

Kris yanks out of the woman's grip. "No. I have to find her. I—"

"We will," Brooke says, unusually calm. Brooke is their wild one. Well, more or less. "But we do it together. As a team."

Kris looks away, then finally nods. It's her fault. All her fault.

She fell asleep when she should've woken Mel up as soon as she began feeling tired.

That's how watch detail works.

Mel has every right to be pissed. Shit, if Tanner was missing, Kris might not have been able to stop herself from killing whoever was on watch detail.

They gather near the smoldering ashes of the fire pit.

Mel, arms crossed, tears standing in her eyes, doesn't look at Kris the entire time.

"First," Brooke says. "We do not split up. We stay together and work as a team. Understood?" Everyone nods, except for Mel. Brooke shoots the captain a glare. "Mel." The woman doesn't respond.

"*Captain*."

Mel, tears trailing down her cheeks, says, "What?"

"Do you understand that we work as a team?"

Mel looks away. "We're wasting time."

Brooke ignores her. "Okay, so, second, we take turns calling for her. Wait ten seconds between shouts. That way, if she calls back, we'll hear her better."

Kris wants to hug Brooke. It's rare that a corporal takes control, and Brooke typically doesn't like to, but…

Then Brooke lifts a tattered piece of red cloth up.

Mel sucks in a quick breath, like she's been slapped.

"I found this by the bushes over there." Brooke points at the cluster of bushes near Mel's tent. "I say we start there and work our way out. If we don't find her by this afternoon, we'll have to—"

"Call the DNR," Kris says. "Cops don't know the woods."

"Right," Brooke says and faces Mel. "Can you do this without going crazy on us, hun?"

Mel just glares at Brooke for a long moment. She says nothing.

"Mel?"

The captain's glare shifts away. "Yeah. Let's go." She turns toward the cluster of bushes.

Kris and Brooke lead Mark and Tanner to the bushes where Mel waits for them.

Mel still won't meet Kris's eyes, even when she says, "Eyes and ears open. All of you. No talking until it's your turn to call for her. Stay together." Then Mel plunges through the bushes without another word.

Brooke nudges Kris. "We need to keep an eye on her."

"Yeah." Kris pushes through the bushes. On the other side, Mel looks like she's about ready to explode. Literally.

Kris keeps her mouth shut. An apology might send Mel further over the edge.

Edge, hell, Kris thinks. *She'd probably shoot me.*

Brooke has them form an arrowhead, a formation Kris knows well.

"This way," Brooke tells Mark and Tanner. "We all get a view of our surroundings better."

"Avery," Mel shouts, taking the immediate lead of the arrowhead formation.

"Well," Brooke says to Kris. "At least we don't have to draw straws or something."

They call in behind Mel. Mark and Tanner at her flanks. Kris and Brooke behind them. Perfect arrowhead. Well, more or less. They walk deeper into the woods.

"AAVERY," Mark shouts.

Tanner waits ten seconds. "Avery!"

Kris still kicks herself for being so stupid.

In all her twelve years in the Army, she never fell asleep on the job, no matter how dead tired she felt.

The woods remain utterly silent around them. No bird song. Nothing.

"AAAVERRRY," Brooke calls.

The only sounds are of them trudging through dead leaves and weeds, of the shouting. Kris listens as Brooke's call fades, then shouts for Avery.

She spots a few tree trunks littered with claw marks and tries to quell the rampaging of her heart.

All of this wouldn't be happening if Kris had just listened to Brooke yesterday. The blame is on Kris, and her stomach churns at the very thought of it. How could she have been so selfish? Even if her reasons weren't, she made the wrong call.

Mel calls, "AAVERRRY!"

But the girl doesn't answer.

Still, Mel on point, they march through Maker's Woods calling and listening. Calling, and listening. They keep their eyes and ears wide open.

Not a single squirrel leaps from branch to branch, nor a bird flits through the colorful canopy.

It's like the woods are dead.

14

"I think we're lost," Mark whispers, too loudly, to Tanner.

"*Shh*," Mel says. Then, "AAAVERRRY!"

Brooke says, "Mel, hun, it's almost five in the afternoon. We need a break."

Mel shakes her head, forges onward.

They all take turns calling for Avery. No answer comes.

"We'll keep searching," Kris says, "but Mark and Tanner need—"

Mel stops so suddenly Mark runs into her. She spins around, glare fixing instantly on Kris. "*You* have no right to speak to me. Not now, or ever." She shoots a glare at Brooke. "We keep moving until we find my baby. Got me?"

Brooke straightens. "No. We all need a break."

Mel turns away. "There are no breaks during a mission."

"During a—Mel, hun, we're not on a *mission*. We're—"

"This *is* a mission and we do not stop until she's found." Mel snaps a glare over her shoulder. "That's an order, Corporal."

Brooke and Kris share a concerned glance, both pale and a little wide-eyed. If Mel gets too much further out of hand, they'll have to do something about it,

"We keep moving," Mel says. "AAAVERRY!"

Kris pulls Brooke aside. "She's going to kill us out here."

Brooke's lips tighten. "You'd be the same way if Tanner was missing. Same here with Mark."

"Right. I get it. But they're just kids," Kris waves a hand at the boys. "We can't force them through this."

For a moment, Brooke is quiet. Finally, she blows out a long sigh and says, "Yeah. But Mel is crazy right now. I don't blame her, but…you should've listened to me, hun."

"I know," Kris says. "I'm an idiot."

"No. I get why. You had good reason. But still…" She watched Mel walk farther and farther away. "Yeah, let's try to convince her to stop for five minutes. At least."

When they catch up with her, Mel is mumbling something under her breath. It takes Kris a while to recognize the words. It's a lullaby.

"Twinkle, twinkle little star…"

"Mel," Brooke says.

But the woman keeps walking. Keeps singing. She breaks away a few thin branches, stomps down pricker bushes, and never stops singing.

Alright. That's enough.

"*Captain*," Kris shouts.

Mel's shoulders twitch. She stops singing, though continues walking.

Kris says, "I'm sorry I fell asleep. I don't know why—"

Mel turns in a single, fluid motion, lifting her rifle so that the muzzle is an inch from Kris's face. The look in Mel's bloodshot, hazel eyes is enough to quicken Kris's heart. She sucks in a breath.

"Whoa, dude," Brooke says. "Really?"

"Thought I told you to shut up." Mel's eyes burn into Kris's.

Kris slowly lifts her arms. "You're really going to shoot me, now? Really?" Her voice barely conceals her unease. No matter how many times she's been shot at, having a gun shoved into her face still scares her a bit.

Mel's glare narrows. "This is all your fault. You—"

A scream slices through Mel's words. Her eyes shift over Kris's shoulder and widen.

"Oh my God," Brooke says.

Mel lowers the gun. Kris spins, freezes in place. All the air whooshes out her. Like a hard fist to the solar plexus.

Tanner screams again, arms flailing, as he's dragged up a tree by his backpack. Something blurry offsets the tree and backpack. Fresh claw marks slash upward. Bits and pieces of bark sift to the ground.

And, just for a second, Kris sees it. A large, scrawny shape with a vulpine head, mouth clamping onto Tanner's backpack.

Slanted green eyes appear to stare directly at her, as if daring her to do something about this. Then it's all blurry again against the tree.

Kris yanks the Smith and Wesson .45 she planned to give Tanner, aims, pulls the trigger.

The thing yelps and drops Tanner. The blur moves up the tree. Luckily, Brooke and Mark are there to somewhat break his fall, which has to be from damn near fifteen feet up.

Kris runs to her son, keeping a close eye on the treetop. The boy shoves Brooke and Mark aside, eyes wild, trying to look everywhere at once. A few pine needles stick in his hair. He makes a strange whiny noise in his throat as he runs away from the tree.

"Tan," Kris says, grabs him.

He screams. Long and loud. He fights her, kicks and scratches, tries to bite her hands.

"Honey," Kris says, struggling to hold him. Her son is like a tangle of vipers. "It's okay. Shh. I got you now. I—"

"Nononononono," Tanner say, shaking his head. "*Run*!"

He twists out of her grip and would've ran off into the woods if not for Mel. Mel, all five-feet-two-inches of her, wrestles the boy to the ground. She holds him there until, eventually, he faints.

Mel makes sure his pulse is strong, then looks at Kris. "He's okay. Just…we have to find Avery and get the hell out of here."

Gone is the craziness from Mel's eyes. Now she just looks tired. Liver-colored crescents hang under each hazel eye. Her cheeks are gaunt, paler than they have any right to be.

Kris kneels and envelopes Mel in her arms. They hug for a moment, then Brooke says, "Ladies, we better haul ass before whatever that was comes back or it gets dark." There's an edge to her voice, something rare to hear from Brooke. Fear, Kris has no doubt.

She feels the same.

15

It takes Tanner five or so minutes to wake up.

He cries out, scrambles away from Kris, eyes darting.

"Hey," she says and reaches for him. "It's okay. *You're* okay."

Closer to the tree than he's supposed to be, Mark says, "Its blood is trying to eat all the bark. Mom, you think I should get a sample of—"

"Dude," Brooke says. "This is your final warning. Stay away from the *trees*."

"But—"

"No buts. Get over here."

Mel shouts, "AAVERRY!"

Tanner, tears in his eyes, says, "I-I wanna go home."

Kris nods. "As soon as we find Avery."

"No! Now. It's going to eat us!"

"It bleeds," she says. "And we have guns. If it attacks again, we'll kill it."

Tanner looks away, tears trickling down his cheeks. He says nothing more. She helps him to up and says, "We'll be home before you know it."

The boy remains silent, following Kris to where Mel, Brook, and Mark wait.

The woods lie motionless, silent, save for a random breeze that rustles the dying leaves. Dry, scratching sounds.

Mel has them form the arrowhead again and they set out.

Tanner, head whipping back and forth, though titled toward the tops of the trees, never calls Avery's name.

It's 5:46 pm.

16

Dusk gives the woods an ethereal golden-green glow Kris doesn't care for.

Any other day, she would love the beauty of it.

Not today.

The glow means night is close. Very close.

And they still haven't found Avery.

She doesn't even know where in the woods they are now.

Maker's Woods isn't the largest forest, by any means, but it's plenty big enough to get lost in for a day or two. And at night…well, Kris feels it'll be damn near impossible to find a way out. Especially with whatever seems to be hunting them now.

She keeps seeing that sleek, black body dragging her son up the tree. Like a leopard hauling its prey onto a high branch. That image keeps shuffling over and over before her mind's eye.

Yeah, they need to get out of the woods before—

"*Avery*? Oh my God!"

Kris snaps back to the here and now. Mel sprints toward the base of a dead tree sticking out of the ground like a jagged, rotten tooth. At first, she doesn't get it, doesn't see why Mel is freaking out. Nothing clicks. Even as her eyes capture everything, her brain refuses to accept the facts. It denies everything because what she sees can't be real.

But it is.

Finally, her brain relents. Wave after noxious wave of acceptance pummels her. A sour lump forms in her throat like moist bread. All the strength drains from her legs. She leans against a nearby elm to keep her balance.

"Oh, *shit*," Brooke says.

"Mom?" Tanner says. He's in front of her, but not enough to obscure her view.

Almost to the dead tree stump, Mel begins to scream. Beyond this is the mouth of large cave draped in dying moss.

Attached to the stump in stuff that resembles yellow spider web, is Avery. Her head is down, dark hair dangling over her face.

It's like something partially cocooned her here, saving her for later; a midnight snack, perhaps.

Mel is pulling on the web-stuff and screaming her daughter's name over and over. She doesn't care what hears her. Or that maybe… Avery is bait and—*shit.*

"*Mel,*" Kris shouts. "Get away from her! I think it's a—"

Something crashes into Mel hard enough to send her flying. She lands in a bed of leaves about ten feet away from the dead tree stump, coughing and slinging curses in Spanish.

Brooke pats Kris's arm, and just like that, she clicks back to herself. A dull cold moves through her.

"Tanner. Mark. Stay here. Shoot anything that comes close. Brooke…c'mon."

Brooke is at her side in an instant. Kris's sight never leaves the blurry figure circling the stump Avery is still fixed to.

"See it?" she asks.

Brooke answers, her voice barely above a whisper. "Yup." She thumbs the safety off her rifle. "Unload on it?"

Kris flicks her safety off too. "When it comes around the other side the stump… Away from Avery."

Cool. Calculated. The same mindset she employs while on any recon mission.

"Right on," Brooke says.

The blurry shape disappears around the tree. Kris lifts her rifle, aiming to the left of the stump where it'll appear again. She blows a slow breath out and waits.

"There." Brooke fires.

Black blood spurts the air and Kris sends bullets into the blur.

There isn't a yelp or scream this time, but a loud, shocked squeal. The blur fades away from it, leaving in its wake a monster with shiny, black skin, a large, hunched back and shoulders, broad head. Its body is like a mashup between a gorilla and a shaved tiger with no ears, though a bit larger than any comparison.

It stumbles, falls flat on its stomach. A weak hissing sound issues from its open mouth. A mouth filled with rows of pointy teeth.

Speechless, face like a sheet of iron, Mel walks over to the creature, pulls her sidearm, and unloads four bullets into its skull.

Kris and Brooke sprint to her. Mel spits on the dead thing and holsters her pistol. Then, using a survival knife, she begins cutting the strange yellow webbing away from Avery.

"Mel?" Brooke ventures.

"Shut up and help me get her out of this shit."

They do as they're told.

The webbing sticks to Kris's hands like flypaper as she cuts and pulls. It also has a cloying smell, like rotting bananas.

They cut enough away from Avery, and the girl slumps forward into Mel's arms. Mel, crying, checks the girl's pulse.

"Okay," Mel says. "She's okay. Just…sleeping." Mel cradles her daughter.

Brooke taps Kris's shoulder. "I need you to take a look at this." She leads her to the dead creature.

The black blood coils around the body.

"This…isn't an animal," Brooke whispers.

Kris's sight slips over its long, black claws. "What is it, do you think?"

"How the hell should I know?"

Kris stares at the face of the thing. Wolfish, yet also with a hint of smooshed feline features. A strange combination, really. "Maybe a government experiment?"

"Or an *alien*," Brooke says. "Either or, we need to tell someone about this, hun."

"Yeah." Kris watches the thing's blood squeeze the body, listens to the bones snap. She turns away, stomach squirming. "I can call General Berk. Maybe he'll know what to do about it."

Brooke says, "Maybe. I say we mark the location and get outta here. Let everyone else figure it out."

"Right." Kris nods at Mel and Avery. Avery has her eyes open, but other than that… "Let's get outta here."

"Had me at get," Brooke says.

She's tying a red bandana on a stick to mark the location when Tanner shouts, "Look!"

Kris and Brooke follow Tanner's finger. They round the large tree stump and…

"Oh…lovely," Brooke says.

Gradually, objects that hadn't been there before materialized. The shimmery green egg-shaped things dangle from the lower tree limbs by the same yellow web-like stuff that held Avery. In the dying light, the objects glitter.

The more Kris takes in the scene, the more she sees. There are dozens of them, with the majority hanging from branches like weird Christmas decorations, though a few lay in piles on the ground.

Beyond all of this, the cave. An opening to darkness.

Large piles of rocks make a rudimentary perimeter around the objects.

"Are those…eggs?" Kris asks no one in particular.

Behind her, Mel says, "We're leaving. Right now."

Beside her, Brooke says, "We should take one back to show General Berk, or whoever. You know? Proof is better than none."

"Berk knows I'm honest," Kris says.

"Sure. But you really think he'll believe *this*?" Brooke spreads her arms out, indicating the entire scene.

It isn't so much about believing, but trust. Still, Brooke, once more, makes a valid point. Proof goes a long way in forcing someone to believe.

Without another word, or Kris's approval, Brooke moves toward the nest, or whatever it is.

Kris grabs her arm. "Wait. There might be more of those creatures around."

The corporal gives Kris a sidelong glance, then stares at the dangling egg and nest. "Maybe it laid all these eggs by itself, though. It's possible."

"I get that, but I wonder how long it's been here, you know? What if these eggs are a second generation, or third?"

"I doubt it's been here that long, Boss. I'm sure someone would've discovered them by now."

Kris knows she's not going to win this one. "But you saw how the eggs just appeared? They're like that thing. Able to blend in with their surroundings. Natural camo."

Brooke falls silent and Kris wonders if maybe she better hog-tie the woman or something. Moments of long silences for Brooke tend to turn out badly, for whatever reason.

The woman surprises her, though. "Okay. Let's just haul ass out of here then."

Kris lets Brooke go and turns to help Mel with Avery. Quick footfalls thump behind her. Mel's eyes widen.

"*Brooke*," Mel shouts.

Kris spins, heart skipping a beat or two. Then she's chasing after her friend.

Somewhere behind her, Mel shouts, "No!"

But orders are moot. Right now, it's about stopping the madness before it sets in.

Brooke stops between two piles of rocks that make up a section of the perimeter. When Kris tries to grab her again, Brooke sidesteps and says, "Listen. We *need* proof."

"I know," Kris says. Her eyes keep trying to look everywhere at once, trying to scan their surroundings. An uneasy thickness fills this small area of the woods. "But…"

"Just one. Look, right there." Brooke points at a cluster of shimmery green eggs no more than four feet from them. "I'll just grab one and we'll leave. Slick as shit down a stripper's pole."

Kris opens her mouth, closes it again. She doesn't know how to respond to this.

"Just wait here," Brooke says and moves carefully beyond the perimeter.

A couple feet from the cluster, slightly to the right, stands a small tree. More eggs sway from its sagging branches.

Soft hissing sounds drift on the breeze. Near the cave, the slightest blur. There and gone.

"Brooke," Kris whispers. "Hey. I think—"

"Shh," Brooke says, bending and reaching for the cluster. "Almost—"

One of the shimmering green eggs from the small tree explodes with a loud pop. Black slime splatters Brooke's right arm.

She straightens, pinwheels, and starts to turn as the black slime crawls up her arm like it's alive.

Pop.

Another dangling egg explodes, splashing more of the stuff on Brooke's leg. It slithers from knee to thigh. She tries to brush off the slime, turns to Kris, eyes near to bulging.

"P-proximities," Brooke manages. And stumbles to Kris.

Behind her, a couple more eggs explode. Black slime sprays the air.

Kris helps Avery up—the girl sways, eyes unblinking—yells for Mark and Tanner to run. She checks on Brooke.

The corporal is brushing at the black slime covering her arm and shoulder. She makes thick grunting noise in her throat. Her eyes, as big as golf balls, find Kris. In them, there's something never really seen in Brooke. Fear. Dangling on the frayed ends of sanity.

The slime leeches to Brooke's neck, coils around. She sucks in a wheezy breath, bottom lip quivering. Tears stream down her cheeks.

Kris makes sure Avery is stable and hurries over to Brooke. She picks up a stick, not really sure what the hell she's going to use it for, but with her rifle slung over her shoulder, she needs *something* in her hands. Honestly, she doesn't want to touch the black stuff.

Brooke shakes her head, dark hair whipping. She whines. Like she's on the verge of screaming. And the black slime, it crawls and slithers over her. It slips under her shirt. It plasters itself over her right cheek. A thin string of the stuff wriggles around her ear. Freaking out, Brooke grabs a handful of the substance and pulls. It stretches like taffy. When she lets go, the slime snaps back onto her skin.

And, shit, it reminds Kris so much about the symbiotes in comic books; how alive and aware it seems, as though it knows its purpose. Perhaps it does.

Breath held, Kris tries to pry the black slime off Brooke's right arm. It latches onto the stick immediately and begins crawling up. She blows the breath out and sucks in a rancid stench that reminds her of the dead opossum Kyle found stuck in a narrow crawlspace a couple years ago.

By the time they got it out, it was a maggot-infested, furry mass of rotten meat. The stench of it made Kris vomit, and Kyle had to double bag it to carry it outside.

Now, Kris's stomach turns like a greasy ball. Hot saliva fills her mouth. She swallows it down with an audible click.

The black stuff spirals up the stick. Now a foot closer to her hands. Now eight inches. Six…

If she holds on too much longer, it'll leech onto her.

She tries to pry the stuff off, but it only stretches and snaps back.

Kris growls. Tendons in her neck bulge. Her biceps tremble. She pulls the stick outward and it cracks, spinning her away. She catches her balance on a tree.

In the nest, behind Brooke, the eggs continue bursting.

Movement near the cave draws Kris's attention. One by one, more creatures appear. Slippery, hunch-backed monsters on all fours that pace back and forth with their heads lowered and green eyes watching, like agitated wolves. There are six of them, as far as Kris can tell.

Brooke screams and drops to her knees. She claws at the black stuff and it wraps around her hands, pulling them to her chest, covering them. The thin tendril that's been playing around her ear now slips inside. Brooke's eyes lock onto Kris. There's no doubt what the look means.

Kill me, it says.

Kris has seen it many times and even had to, unfortunately, honor the requests under dire circumstances.

Not Brooke. How the hell is she supposed to kill her best friend?

She can't. She just…*can't.*

There has to be another way…

Then Tanner pulls on her arm. He yells at her to run. He's crying. And she wants to run. She wants to move. But Brooke, those wide, pleading eyes…

Mel says, "*Kris*! They're coming!"

Her sight lifts to the sleek, black, hunchbacked beasts. They jump from rock pile to rock pile around the nest as the eggs continue exploding.

Brooke, on her knees, opens her mouth to either say something or scream and the black slime slithers in. All of it. All at once. She pitches forward, eyes rolling back to reveal only the whites. Kris catches her before she falls on her face.

The monsters, they're closing in, trying to flank her on the right and left.

Kris hauls Brooke to her feet, slaps her. The woman blinks, hand cupping her cheek.

"*Hey*. What—?"

"*Move*," Kris says, nodding at the creatures on the rock piles like horrible gargoyles.

"Shit," Brooke says, seeing the things. She glances at herself. "Where'd it go…?"

"Tell ya later," Kris says, pulling Brooke with her.

They back away, Brooke leaning on Kris until she regains her balance. The closest creature rumbles out a growl, bearing long, pointy teeth. Silvery drool strings from its jutting jaw. It lowers a bit, readying itself to pounce.

A gunshot deafens Kris. A small black hole appears, smoldering, in the monster's slanted forehead. It tumbles off the rock pile. The others glance at the body, and then shoot green glares at Kris. She risks a look over her shoulder. Mel lowers the rifle and nods at Kris. Beside her, Avery looks around, blinking, like she just woke up from a nightmare. In a sense, she has.

"Go," Kris says to Brooke. They spin. "Go!" She waves at Mel and the kids to run.

They do, Avery stumbling at first, then breaking into an awkward sprint. Mark and Tanner try to grab her, but she rushes by, dodging them.

"Avery," Mel cries, as all three kids crash into the brush in front of her.

Kris, gripping Brooke's hand, says, "I'll be right behind you."

Brooke frowns. "Wait, what?"

Kris releases her hand and nods to the woods where the others ran. "Go. I'll be right behind you."

She turns, unslinging her rifle and aiming the muzzle at the first creature she sees.

It comes at her fast and low, kicking up dirt in a brackish cloud behind it. Its green eyes flash.

Kris pulls the trigger, sending a bullet into one of those green eyes. Black blood shoots out the back of its head, dropping the monster. The momentum carries it to a stop a few inches from Kris's boots, its thin, obsidian body twitching.

She backs up a few feet, eyes shifting left to right, up and down, searching for movement. The other creatures are gone. This little section of the woods has fallen still again, like a breath caught in a swollen throat. Even the eggs stop popping.

The dead one in front of her oozes its blood onto the ground. As before with the other, the blood moves and coils around the body. A thin tendril, however, slithers toward her, the tip of it rising and falling, like a snake scenting its prey.

Kris kicks dirt at it and backs away.

"They went into the cave."

Kris clamps her lips shut against a scream. She turns, blows out a harsh breath, and says, "Damn it, Brooke."

The woman shrugs. "What?"

"You were supposed to go with everyone else," Kris says, fighting to keep her tone neutral and failing.

"Yeah, well, I figured I'd hang back and make sure you'd be okay."

"Fine," Kris says. "Let's get out of here."

Brooke winks. "See, I knew you were cool."

17

Mel and the kids wait for them in the clearing where the blinds are set up. The proverbial meadow.

Mel glances from Brooke to Kris, and back again. Her eyes hold Kris's gaze for a moment.

A look that seems to say, *It's inside her.*

Kris gives the tiniest shrug when Brooke hurries to Mark and pummels him with kisses and hugs. Mel's lips form a pale line across her face.

And although Mark smiles, Kris notes an awkwardness to him. It's in his eyes, a hint of worry and, maybe, fear.

He saw the black slime on his mom, but didn't know about it slipping inside of her.

Kris pulls Mel aside and whispers, "What are we gonna do with her?"

"I don't know," Mel says. Her face pales considerably in a grimace, like she's about to vomit. She lowers her head, frowning, driven to thought. The old telltale worry line forms between her eyes.

From Kris's experience, the line means either to look out because the little woman is pissed, or she's legitimately worried and deep in thought.

Finally, Mel says, "We need to turn her over to General Berk. Maybe he'll have connections to help her."

Kris leads Mel further away from the group. "Or they'll cut her into tiny *pieces*. There has to be another way."

"Like what?" Mel shakes her head. "She has…some alien thing inside her. We can't—"

"Whatcha guys doing' over here all by yourselves?"

Even Mel jumps a little.

Brooke smiles and looks from Kris to Mel. Her smile is too big to be genuine.

"Um," Kris says, then sighs. "Okay, look. That black stuff that was all over you? It's *inside* you now."

Brooke lifts an eyebrow. "No. It fell off."

"Hun," Kris says. "We both saw it go into your mouth."

For an instant, maybe a heartbeat, Brooke appears scared. Her eyes widen and she draws in a slow breath.

Then the big smile reclaims her face. She snorts. "You ladies are *good.* Almost had me there."

"It's true," Mel says.

"Mom?"

They all turn. Tanner, Mark, and Avery blink at them.

"Can we go now?" Tanner asks. "Those things are…" He closes his mouth, looks off across the clearing.

All three women look at each other. No one speaking.

It's what they do. A sort of telepathy thing. There's no discussing the matter, anyway.

Kris takes in the surrounding woods. If the creatures followed, there's no sign. But that's not for certain. They can camouflage themselves very well.

Unlike before, now she feels watched. Hunted. Good hunters observe their prey before the kill. They learn their habits, waiting for just the right moment.

They watch…and wait.

Almost to camp, Avery says, "Do we have to pack everything? I just want to go." She seems to be doing a little better. Her terror and shock retreating one step at a time. Like Tanner.

Maker's Woods is as silent as ever.

Kris breathes in the musty odors of bark and dead leaves.

"No," Mel answers her daughter. "Just grab personal things. We're bugging out."

Ahead of Kris, Brooke staggers to the left, then the right. She catches her balance, shakes her head.

"Hey." Kris places a hand on Brooke's shoulder.

The woman stops, turns a bit. "Yeah, Boss?"

"You okay?"

The woman gives her a thumbs up and follows the others into the campsite.

Kris takes a moment to scan the woods behind them, eyes drifting over brambles and tall weeds, though a majority of her focus is on the treetops and branches. She cranes her neck, searching from branch to branch at every tree.

A few dead leaves flutter down from the oak tree at her two o'clock.

Her eyes narrow. She waits.

When nothing happens, she turns and joins everyone in camp.

18

Kris is slinging her duffle bag over the shoulder opposite the one with her rifle, when someone screams.

She drops the bag, heart stuttering.

Outside the tent, Tanner shouts, “Mom!”

She bursts out of the tent. “What…?” Her sight finds Brooke writhing on the ground, Mark on one side, Mel on the other.

Moving closer, Kris asks, “What’s wrong?”

Tanner is behind the fallen tree. He says, “I don’t know. She just fell down and started screaming.”

Kris hops over the tree and kneels beside Brooke. On the other side, Mel’s wide eyes.

“She said her stomach hurt,” Mark says. He’s holding her hand. Gripping. Tears squiggle down his chubby cheeks.

Kris leans close to Brooke. “Hey, hun. We’re gonna get you to a hospital. Can you w—?”

Brooke arches. A loud wail rips out of her mouth. It’s at this exact moment when Kris notices Brooke’s stomach bulge upward. For a few seconds, the woman looks thirty weeks pregnant. Then her stomach flattens again.

“We need to move her,” Mel says. “With all of us, we can carry her back to the vehicle.”

“Right,” Kris says and begins working her hands under Brooke’s shoulders.

A deep popping noise ripples out of Brooke’s body. She arches again, sobbing. Tendons in her neck stick out. Sweat beads her forehead. Her free hand claws the dirt while the other squeezes Mark’s so tight he cries out in pain, but doesn’t try to pull away. Still, Mel pries Brooke’s hand off of his, revealing several shallow, bloody crescents in his skin.

Brooke screams again, but this time it’s louder, shriller. Inhuman. A thin, black tentacle licks out of her mouth then slips back down her throat.

Kris scrambles away, heart whip-cracking. Chill after icy chill shivers through her.

"What—did you see that?" Mel asks, pulling Mark away.

"Yeah," Kris manages through numb lips.

The bulge in Brooke's stomach stretches upward, descends. Shrieking, entire body a series of violent quakes, Brooke rolls onto her stomach. Vomit spurts from her mouth.

Amid all of this, Mark screams.

Kris stands, mind reeling, and pulls the pistol from its holster on her hip. Tanner's pistol.

"What are you *doing*?" Mark starts forward. Mel holds him back.

Truth is, she doesn't know. As she watches her best friend writhe in agony, as Brooke's belly moves and bulges, Kris just doesn't know what to do. She's riding instincts. That black slime is inside Brooke. Maybe it's eating her from the inside out? Killing her. But maybe they can still extract the stuff. They need to—

"K-kill me," Brooke says in a creaky tone. Her eyes hold Kris's. "P-Please."

Kris looks at Mel. Mel looks away. Mark shakes his head, sniffling.

Behind her, Tanner says, "No, Mom."

Brooke's eyes are nothing but black squiggles now. "Kill…me."

Hot tears prickle, blurring Kris's vision. The hand holding the gun trembles. Her stomach cramps up, forcing her to bend a little.

Needle-thin black tentacles slither out of Brooke's nostrils. More wriggle out of her gaping mouth. The black squiggles in her eyes snake out of the corners and squirm along the sides of her face.

Brooke's body shudders, falls still, save for the bulges and tentacles. Soft, but there, Kris hears a long breath whistle out of her friend's mouth. Another doesn't follow.

Kris closes her teary eyes, and pulls the trigger.

The rapport cracks through camp, echoes through the woods. A noise so sudden and loud, even the trees appear to twitch in shock.

When Kris opens her eyes, there's a hole in Brooke's forehead.

"*Noo*!" Mark breaks free of Mel's grip and skids to his knees at his mom's side. He reaches out to touch her.

Kris slaps his hand away from Brooke's face, which writhes with all of those thin tentacles. She shakes her head at him, swallows down a lump in her throat.

Tears dampened face stares up at her, Mark says, "You killed my *mom*!"

"I…"

Mel pulls Mark away. He struggles, though feebly, and ends up burying his face in her shoulder. He ratchets out sobs. Mel holds him, one hand stroking the back of his head. Her eyes find Kris's, then lower to Brooke.

A series of thick popping sounds lift from the body. Another black tentacle peeks out of the bullet hole in Brooke's head.

Kris turns away, grimacing.

She's seen some horrors in her day, but this…this is different. This isn't human.

When she looks again, the bulge in Brooke's stomach spreads until her entire torso is swollen. Like she gained one hundred pounds in two seconds.

Mel pulls on Kris. She's shouting at her to move, telling her they need to go. They need to leave right now!

But Kris can't move. Her legs turn to ice pillars, and no matter how much her brain wails at her to move, she just can't. Even when Tanner joins Mel in pulling on her, the ice refuses to thaw.

A wet, ripping sound comes from Brooke. Her body lolls back and forth.

"*Sergeant*," Mel shouts. "Move your ass! Now!"

Hundreds of small, black tentacles spike out of Brooke's skin, their tips wiggling.

A low groan flows out of Brooke's open mouth.

Then the skin of the woman's stomach stretches outward, from side to side, as if something is trying to dig its way out of her. The tentacles slice a gash down her torso.

Mel slaps her. Hard. The shock of it snaps Kris out of her reverie. She looks at Mel.

"Move, soldier," Mel orders, yanking on Kris's arm.

She stumbles as the ice in her legs thaw, finally melting.

"Mom," Avery says. "Wha—what's…?" She's pointing at Brooke.

Kris does a double take and swallows down vomit.

Brooke rips open from collarbone to groin. A wet, bubbly sound. The small tentacles spill out over the sides, and a claw about the size of a five-year-old's hand reaches out of Brooke's mutilated body.

Mark and Avery scream. Mel barks orders. Kris grabs Tanner by the arm.

This is all it takes.

They sprint toward the far end of camp, in the direction of Kris's Explorer.

Kris spots the slight blur in front of the brush too late. Mark and Avery are slammed to the ground, the blurry shape on top of them.

Mel skids to a stop, lifts her rifle, and squeezes off a shot.

The thing squeals and leaps off the kids. The natural camouflage dissipates and a hunch- backed creature like the other ones charges at Mel.

Kris sidesteps around Mel, draws the .45, and pumps two bullets into its face. Black blood sprays, barely missing Mel, and the monster drops dead.

"There's…more of them," Mel says, pointing at several blurry shapes creeping along the edges of camp.

Mel and Kris round the kids up so they're all together.

"Get your shotguns ready," Kris tells them and returns her attention to the things tracing the perimeter. The treetops seem clear, but looks can be deceiving.

It's 7:58 pm.

19

"Getting dark," Mel says as the blurry creatures circle.

Kris goes quiet. Thinking. Then she says, "We shoot as many as we can and make a run for it."

She gives Brooke's body a glance.

Whatever ripped out of her is gone now. It somehow slipped away without anyone knowing.

It stings, seeing the remains of her best friend. This isn't how anyone should die, let alone someone you love like a sister. Someone who was a hero.

She wipes tears away and focuses her sorrow, pressuring it into rage and hate.

"Wish I had my M4," Mel says. "Or some grenades."

"Or a damn M16," Kris says.

"Or—"

They drop from the trees into camp behind the group. Kris spins, firing twice and missing both times. Dirt sprays in front of one of the monsters as its camo flickers away.

"Shit," she says, aims, and pulls the trigger.

The thing moves just enough and the bullet misses its head, burying itself into the hunched shoulders. It cries out, drops, and scrambles back onto all fours and charges at Kris.

BOOM.

In an instant, the thing's entire face is obliterated in a spray of black gore. It plops onto the ground, twitching.

"Got him, Mom," Tanner says behind her.

"Thank you," she says, swelling with pride.

Mel says, "They're surrounding us. Flanking on all sides."

"Shoot anything that moves," Kris shouts and blasts three rounds into another creature.

The camp fills with gunshots as each of them fight to live.

Kris ejects a clip, slaps a fresh one in. The other two clips are in the duffle bag… The duffle bag still in the tent where she dropped it.

Mark is screaming, moving away from the group. His twelve gauge thunders. Kris risks a look. She watches him turn a monster's head into so much splatter and—

Something slams into her left side, kicking her off her feet. She falls hard on the ground, shell-shocked. Kris has time enough to gain her knees when a hollow hiss blows into her face, fluttering her hair. The smell is like something dead turning to chunky soup in the hot summer sun. She tilts her head up a bit and all the strength drains away. Her mouth opens.

Green eyes narrow. Long, pointy teeth inches from her face click together. Nostril slits flare, taking in air and blowing it out into her sweaty face. Silvery drool patters on the ground.

Three quick gunshots. Mel shouts, "Get up, soldier!"

The monster rears, shrieking, and scrambles away.

Kris stands, fires two shots into the thing. One bullet grazes the top of its head. Black blood streams the air. The other bullet catches it in the chest.

Mel says, "We'll be out of ammo before we make a run for it. There's too many."

A quick glance and Kris knows how horribly right her captain is. The sleek, black creatures are everywhere now. So many more than she realized earlier.

Instead of six or seven, there's roughly a more than a dozen. Maybe more.

Avery blows a black hole into the side of one. She's crying, Kris notices. Crying, but strong enough to fight. She's definitely her mother's daughter. Mark is roaring with all kinds of rage, firing erratically, wasting too many shells on poor shots. She'll need to keep an eye on him. Tanner is down on one knee, picking his shots. Cool and steady. Just like Kyle taught him.

A crescendo of hisses and growls fill the world behind her. She turns. Three of the creatures, heads lowered, move toward her.

Kris takes them down with quick, precise shots to the head.

Dead leaves rain down around the group. Above, blurry shapes creep.

"Trees," Kris shouts.

"On it," Mel says, holsters her sidearm, and lifts the rifle. "Everyone move back."

Kris has to practically drag Mark away from the spot, but he eventually relents as Mel aims and squeezes off a few shots.

Dead things fall from the trees, thudding on the ground near Kris and the kids.

"Right flank," Mel yells.

A monster as big as a Great Dane crashes into her, driving her to the ground. Dirt clouds suffocate the air around her.

Long, black claws dig into her shoulders. The beast growls into Kris's face. Its talons sink into her skin. Pain surges through her in awful brilliance. Almost paralyzing. A scream rips out of her. She's been hurt before. Shot more than once. But this pain…it's deeper, somehow. A constant sting radiating and pulsing through the nervous system.

Then the monster's razor-lined maw opens.

***

Satellite images aren't enough to convince General Berk. Even with the special military scope, which reveals clearer images than the civilian lenses.

It's the thermal scans of the region that sends a ping of unease through him. Over fifty vague heat signatures and five strong ones. The vague signatures are oddly shaped. Nothing in the region resembles them, according to his Chief Analyst Becca Roberts.

What was it she told him?

The body structures appear both wolf-like and feline? And larger than both?

"There are people, too," Becca says, circling the stronger cluster of heat signatures. "Right there." She looks at Berk, then shifts her gaze to the other officers. "I believe these people are in trouble."

Jack Miller, Director of Homeland Security, leans forward, elbows on the table. "Are you saying this is some sort of alien invasion, Ms. Roberts?"

She shakes her head. "No, though I'm not quite sure at this point." Her attention drifts to Berk. "But I do know something extraordinary is happening right now that deserves our attention."

Berk leans back in his chair, a deep frown creasing his face.

Thinking.

20

Kris drives a knee into the thing's stomach.

It grunts and moves away just enough for her to get the pistol between them. She pulls the trigger. The bullet blasts out the back of its head, splattering black blood in every direction. All of it completely missing Kris and everyone else, thankfully.

The monster is heavy, like trying to push a three-hundred-pound man off her. She manages to roll it to the side and squirm out.

The camp is dim, the sun retreating as night sinks its teeth in.

The things are hard enough to fight in the daylight.

"We gotta run for it," Kris says to Mel.

Around them lay more than a dozen dead creatures.

"How?" Mel unloads the rest of her clip into a two nearby monsters, ejects, slaps a fresh one in. "They're everywhere. And this is my last clip."

Tanner loads five more shells into his shotgun.

Avery says, "I don't have any more shells!"

Mark, though, he's blasting away and screaming. All rage. He has to be really close to being out, too.

"It's almost night," she says to Mel. "We can't fight them in the dark."

Mel takes out two more of the hunch-backed creatures and faces Kris. "Then we better find a place to hide until morning."

But where do you hide from monsters like these?

Kris fires and shears off the side of a wolfish face. A place surfaces in her mind.

"Plains Waterfall," she says. "There's a cave behind it."

Mel frowns, then her eyes widen. She nods.

"You lead," Kris says. "I'll keep 'em off our backs." She takes Tanner's shogun and his remaining ten shells, which she stuffs into her pockets. "Follow Mel," she tells her son.

Tanner opens his mouth to protest, then shuts it. He moves closer to Mel.

Avery, seeing this, follows Tanner. But Mark…

He's wailing, blasting monsters away, though he misses more than he hits the targets. He's wasting ammo now.

A claw whisks the air in front of her. Kris drops to the side, turns, and pumps two bullets into the chest of a hunch-backed monster. She straightens and nudges him.

"Hey, we're—"

Mark spins, the twelve-gauge muzzle now an inch from Kris's face. Down the barrel, on the opposite end of the gun, Mark sobs. His eyes fill with tears, break free, and squiggle down his chubby cheeks.

"You…" he says in a raspy voice. "You killed her. You…" His lips quiver, twisting to form words, failing.

"Your mom was in a lot of pain, hun," Kris says. "Suffering."

"So? Y-you *killed* her!"

Kris snatches the gun out of Mark's hands. He slumps, crying. Giving up.

"You…you killed her," he repeats over and over.

"I had to," Kris says, trying to hold back her own tears and failing. The fact that Brooke had already been dead, or close to it when Kris pulled the trigger doesn't matter.

A mom is dead.

A friend is dead.

And what about the thing that came out of her body? Where'd it go? Is this how those monsters breed?

Kris says, "Mark, honey, I'm sorry. But we have to run now. Okay? I loved your mom, too."

He wipes tears from his cheeks, and joins Tanner and Avery.

"Ready?" Mel calls.

The creatures move closer, forming a U-shape around the group from the rear. Kris hands Mark back his shotgun and says, "Shoot only what you know you can kill."

He sniffles, nods.

Then she turns to the monsters. In the dying light, they snap their pointy teeth at her. Hisses fill the air like thousands of pit vipers. Green eyes glow, all of them on her as she steps away from the others.

"When you are, Cap," Kris says and uses Tanner's shotgun to blow three of the creature's heads off in two shots.

"Follow me, kids," Mel says and runs into the woods.

The kids follow, leaving Kris behind.

A few of the creatures lift their heads as Mel and the kids flee. Kris whistles at them, and their focus returns to her, pummeling her again and again with their hunger and hate.

Blood ticks in her throat.

The monsters begin to close the gap.

***

"We don't even know if she's right, Paul," Jack Miller says as he paces back and forth in front of Berk's desk.

"The images are enough for me," Berk says. "I'm sending in a team to locate and rescue those people."

Jack stops, runs a hand through his thinning, black hair. "And what about the threat? Could be a terrorist attack. Maybe they're wearing cloaks or—"

Berk interrupts with a chuckle. "*Cloaks*? This isn't science fiction, Director."

"I know that." Jack's face reddens a bit. "What I mean is, you're seriously convinced we might be dealing with hostile aliens?"

Berk shakes his head. "I don't know what we're dealing with here, but we're going to deal with it. The teams will be dropped off closer to the people. Another team will be sent to eradicate and bag whatever is out there."

"Don't you think we should wait, first? Observe closer? Study them—?"

Berk slams a fist on his desk. "No." He stands and points a finger at Jack. "Last I checked, I'm in charge here. And this how I'm taking care of the problem. Don't like it? Take it up with the president."

"But I—"

"Get the hell out of my office, Director."

Jack straightens his suit, clears his throat, and leaves.

“Prissy little shit,” Berk mutters to himself and picks up his phone. He presses a green button and waits a moment.

Then…

“Deploy.”

21

She shoots as many as she can before the shotgun is empty, shredding through six of the hunch-backed beasts.

Black blood, it slithers everywhere and consumes the bodies.

Something presses against the toe of her boot. In the dimness, she sees a black tendril oozing onto her boot. She kicks, and thankfully, the stuff flies off. It splatters into the face of an approaching monster. The beast roars and claws at its face, trying to get the blood off.

The others look at their injured brethren.

Kris takes the moment to run.

She whirls and sprints through the gathering darkness of night. There's no sign of Mel and the kids.

She knows where Plains Waterfall is, but at night…

A bunch of shrieks and hisses erupt behind her but she doesn't stop, hoping they can't see so well at night. They probably do, though. One of them got Avery, after all. At night.

The moon isn't full, but it casts just enough light for her not to be totally drenched in darkness.

She runs, dodging trees, leaping over the brambles that she's able to see. Somewhere around here, there's a narrow ravine. Even in the day, it sneaks up on a person. Kris bursts through a patch of pricker bushes. The tiny thorns shred parts of her jeans. Pain laces up and down her legs.

Something crashes through the brush behind her. Not far.

Were they using the trees, too?

If so, they might drop down on her at any moment and she'd be dead.

Faint, she thinks she hears the *wupwupwup* of a helicopter.

But that can't be. No one knows they're out here. And even is someone does, it's not like Kris and everyone are late getting home. Kris's mom won't worry until a couple days of not answering the phone, and she knows Kris is out here with Tanner for the weekend.

So, no, that can't be a helicopter.

She comes to the hulking glow of Ghost Rock, a huge, random boulder Kris named herself during a hike with Brooke a few years ago.

Maker's Woods got its name honestly. Or not so much, depending on one's view or beliefs.

When this tiny section of Iowa was settled in 1723, the woods had no name. Just a place to get trees for lumber and hunt for food. I wasn't until people began turning up missing, or dead, a few years later that the thick woods north of the small community—known then as Johnson's Hold—got its name.

Suicides, mostly; bodies found hanging from trees by hunters, bodies found on the ground. Sometimes it was a kid. Sometimes an adult. Over two hundred deaths since the land was settled, and those were found. Many more remain missing till this day. Thus, people dubbed the town and woods Maker's. As in, Meet Your Maker.

As Kris plows through the dark woods, monsters practically nipping at her heels, she can't help but recall why she named the random boulder Ghost Rock. Mainly because the memory has Brooke in it.

It's limestone, though it's turned a pale gray over the centuries it's been there. Thick swaths of green moss spot it here and there. Indeed, it has the appearance of some ancient dead thing. Long forgotten by even time itself.

But its appearance played a minor role in its naming.

While resting one day by the boulder, Kris and Brooke noticed something odd near its base, wrapped in a tangle of a wild rose bush. When they checked it out, spreading the tangles a bit, Kris saw a human skull, or part of one anyway. Then, sort of curled around the base of the boulder, the entire skeleton. Freaked them both out a little, but in the end, they decided to leave the remains of whoever it was undisturbed and unreported. For good or ill, or whatever reason, the owner of the skeleton chose to die next to the old boulder. Maybe they thought they'd be found easier, since the thing was so random.

No one had, though, until Kris and Brooke stumbled across it.

So…with the deadness of the boulder and real death at its base, Kris named it Ghost Rock. And whatever haunted it, surely rested at its feet.

The *wupwupwup* of the helicopter grows louder, yet, Kris can't stop to try to signal.

Creatures that have no right to exist on this earth chase her. If she doesn't find Plains Waterfall soon, they'll get her.

And she's getting winded. Not bad yet, but her lungs are beginning to burn and her heart rate is kicking into overdrive.

A hiss sounds directly behind her. Something wickers through her hair, taking a few strands with it.

She cries out, pushing herself to run faster. She drops the shotgun to lighten her load, to run faster. It's not working.

The *wupwupwup* fades, and Kris is once more alone. Any thoughts of rescue dash to the wayside.

The moonlight angles through the trees just enough to spot the sharp drop off of the narrow ravine.

She jumps across with no trouble.

Now she hears the sound of falling water. Not far at all now.

Plains Waterfall isn't the largest, but if she can sneak behind it, there's a small cave. The water will mask their scent. At least she hopes so.

But as she nears the sound of the waterfall, she also notes the noises of snapping limbs and hisses behind her. If she goes behind the waterfall with the creatures so close, they'll no doubt follow.

Easy picking for the beasts.

Gotta shake 'em off, somehow, she thinks.

She could lead them away, shoot a couple, double back, but still, there's a chance one or more will follow.

That's when someone shouts, "Get down!"

And the night explodes with gunfire.

DEEP IN THE CAVE

She's had many offspring since waking up in this strange, new place, and until now, she has left the creatures that walk upright alone. She saw a mild threat in the uprights, but not food, nor strong enough to provide viable offspring.

Since her arrival, it has watched the uprights kill the animals for food and sport, or just walk around. None of them bothered her, or her pups, so she let them be as well.

Then, this new group of uprights came…

They hurt one of her pups, so she took one of theirs. Not to eat, but in anger.

Then they killed more pups to get theirs back. Now all of her pups were out to kill them all.

Yes, she has had many offspring during its time here, but none like the thing that crawls into the cave, mewling.

It was born from an upright, and its shape, even its scent, is different. The way it moves, on odd hind legs and long front legs that remind its mother of the uprights; it's like a spider.

There's a moment where she almost kills this peculiar pup, but only briefly.

Instincts overpower the mother. There is a deep connection only shared between mother and offspring; an undeniable force, a bittersweet tether.

It mewls, nudges her with its angular head, much the same way the other pups have done.

So, accepting this new pup, she coaxes it in for cuddling. The pup snuggles close and she is surprised at how hot it feels against her skin. It's nearly unbearable, yet, she doesn't move away.

The pup begins to purr and, content, she closes her eyes.

She doesn't even feel the tentacle slither around her neck until it's too late.

Until it cinches tight.

22

Lights flash into her face, shift away.

All around her, people are setting up equipment and high-density lights.

"You're safe now, miss," a man says and helps her up.

Kris looks around, stunned. "What…who…?"

"US Marine Force Recon, miss," says the soldier. He's about an inch taller than her with cool, blue eyes. "I'm Lieutenant Riley."

She nods. "Sergeant Kristin Jenson. Army Special Ops."

He salutes her. He outranks her, but there's respect. "Didn't know we had a soldier here, ma'am."

Kris shrugs. She can't think of anything to say. Can't really think at all right now.

Perhaps noticing this inability, Lt. Riley says, "Our medic wants to take a look at your wounds."

"Wounds…?"

He points at her shoulders where there are holes in her jacket and splotches of blood.

"Oh." She almost forgot about those. Of course, remembrance brings with it pain.

She eyes two soldiers dressed in black as they bag one of the creatures.

"Did you…did you get them all?"

"Yes, ma'am."

"Did you check the trees?"

"This area is secure, ma'am."

Kris nods. "Okay."

The medic, a short man maybe in his early thirties, hurries over, and has her sit while he inspects the wounds.

"Punctures," he says, mostly to himself. "Not too deep, though. I'll clean 'em and patch ya up."

"Fantastic," she says, then glances around. "Where's Mel and the kids?"

"What?" He pours on roughly a gallon of alcohol.

Kris chokes back a scream as her skin feels like it's been set on fire.

When the burning and stinging passes, she says, "My friend, Captain Melanie Hernandez, and three kids."

"We only found you, ma'am."

"Plains Waterfall," Kris blurts. "That's where they are. We have to get them."

"I'll let Lieutenant Riley know."

"Or you can give me your M4 and I'll get them myself."

"Um, ma'am, I know you outrank me, but I have my order to—"

"My son is in danger right now, *medic*."

He blinks at Kris then catches the attention of Lt. Riley.

Riley frowns, walks over, and asks, "Yes?"

Before the medic can respond, Kris says, "My son is still out there. I've got to go find him."

"Negative, Sergeant. I have orders to secure the area and rescue the victims. I will send my men out as soon as these things are on ice—"

Kris yanks the M4 from the medic and points it at Lieutenant Riley. "I'm gonna say this one more time. My *son* is out there, not far to the south of here, and I need to find him. Understand?"

"Yes, but—"

"Is that understood, *sir*?"

Riley lowers his gaze and says, "I'll have to report this."

"Do it," Kris says and adds, "Give me a grenade, two more mags, and night vision."

"I can't—"

"Please, Lieutenant. I'm not asking as a soldier. I'm asking as a mother who needs to find her son. There's more of those things out there. So either come with me now, or give me the things I need."

Riley sighs. "Okay. Fine. Giver her your gear, Reynolds."

The medic, stone-faced, hands over a grenade, two magazines for the M4, and a pair of new night vision goggles.

"Thank you," Kris says, trying to find a place on her body to hold it all.

"Here," Medic Reynolds says and takes off his belt and hands it over. He keeps his sidearm.

Kris buckles the belt tight, stows the mags in their spot, and pockets the grenade. She fits the goggles to her head.

"I'll be back," she says.

"You have an hour before we pack up and move to a different site," Lieutenant Riley says. He lowers his voice just a bit. "I hope you find him."

Kris nods and runs out of the secure area.

23

She has to readjust herself to seeing through night vision goggles.

It's been awhile… Like years.

But as all things one has done before, it comes back like riding a bike.

Kris stops every so often to check the trees and her surroundings. If the creatures are using their camo, she probably won't see them, of course. Just something she has to take into account.

Maker's Woods is motionless, though. Not even a breeze.

With night slips in the chill of autumn, though she barely feels it. Her heart pumps blood too hard and adrenaline kicks her core body temperature up a few degrees.

With the night vision, it doesn't take long to find Plains Waterfall.

"Mel," she says, working her way over the large rocks around a small spring pond the falls empties into. "Hun, I'm here."

The waterfall tumbles from a thirty-foot cliff. Kris suspects it's more like fifty feet, though. The water is all spring fed. Brooke and Kris liked to stop here for a drink of cold water. Not from the pond, but fresh out of another spring nearby.

She presses her back against the cliff and inches toward the waterfall. Through the goggles, she can see a foot or so of space between the falling water and face of the cliff.

Kris shouts, "Mel?" Moves closer. "It's me, hun."

No answer.

Her heart quickens. What if they didn't make it to the waterfall? What if—?

"Kris?" Mel's face appears in the space between waterfall and cliff. If not for the night vision, Kris wouldn't see her at all.

Relief spills through Kris. "Yeah. It's me. Everyone okay?"

"We're fine. What took you so long? You were supposed to be right behind us."

"They—I'll explain later. There's a recon team here."

"Recon?" Mel frowns. "Berk?"

"Maybe," Kris says. "I dunno how he knows about what's going on here, though."

"Satellites," Mel says. "Okay, kids, let's get out of here."

"Mom?" Tanner's voice ignites a flame inside Kris.

"I'm here, kiddo. Come on. We gotta hurry."

One at a time, they inch out from behind the waterfall.

They gather on the rocks.

Then gunfire shatters the silence.

***

The area is secure, and Lieutenant Mark Riley prides himself on getting it done efficiently. Saving Sergeant Jensen, though, that was their primary objective: Saving the people who are trapped here. And although he might get some heat from General Berk, letting her go to find her son made more sense than keeping her here to wait for their orders to go in search. She'd be a nervous wreck the entire operation. And besides, she's trained. Special Ops. Not like she doesn't know what she's doing.

He watches his men pack another creature in ice bags. Sleek, hunch-backed black beasts. No word yet if they're alien or mutants of some sort. All he knows is they're a high priority right now.

After the woman left, he talked to General Berk. The operation is a success and they are to rendezvous with Red Team a mile northwest. That's if their leader, Brett Morgan, ever answers his damn radio. Riley never liked that prick, anyway. The plan is: Meet at rendezvous point, load the bags, and return to base. A sanitation crew will be out in the morning.

Riley sighs and checks the time.

The sergeant has about twenty minutes.

He glances at the darkness beyond the high-density lights. Thinking maybe he should send a couple of his guys out there to bring her—and if there are still others—back safely.

Then someone screams. The area becomes a chaotic mess.

"*East*," Private Pedro shouts.

Through the bud in his ear, Private Wilkes says, "Sir, we have a breach on the east—no wait—*south* side of—"

Static fills Riley's ear.

He hisses, pulls the earbud out, and catches his next in command, Corporal Mills, by the arm.

Mills struggles, wild-eyed.

"What is it?" Riley practically has to shake the kid.

Mills, he says, "Not like the other, sir. It's…it's…"

Gunfire lights up the night. First on the east side, then south, back to east.

"What is it?" someone shouts.

"It's over here!" someone else yells.

"It got Anderson!"

"Where's Williams?"

Mills wrenches out of Riley's grip and runs into the woods.

Cordite chokes the air. His men are running around acting like scared teenagers instead of—

"*Marines*," Riley roars.

The men pause, but only for a few seconds. They cluster to the cast, firing into the woods, and move to the south, then west.

"It's *everywhere*," one of his men, Sullivan, he thinks, cries. "Can't get a lock on it."

Riley storms to the command post where Private Johnson still sits. His eyes are so large Riley almost expects them to literally pop out of their sockets.

"Hey," Riley says, snaps his fingers in front of Johnson's face.

The man blinks, looks at Riley. "You see this?"

"See what? I—"

"Here," Johnson points at one screen. "And here." Points at another. "There." Points back at the first screen again.

Riley gets it. He sees. Watches the red mass flicker out in one screen and appear in the next.

"What the…?"

"This ain't like those other things in the bags, sir. They had low body temps, but consistent. This…it's something else, I think."

Riley watches it flickers back and forth between screens. He listens to his men scream or bark orders at each other.

"Radio Berk. Let him know what's going on and have Red Team port here immediately."

"Copy," Johnson says. "But Red Team has been unresponsive since we deployed."

"Try," Riley says. "We need—"

Long, black tentacles lash out of the darkness, wrap around Palmer's and Roger's necks, and yank them into the woods.

Now the screaming trumps the orders and almost overpowers the chugs of machine guns.

His team is disintegrating before his eyes. Marines, as tough as they come, reduced to screaming as whatever is out there picks them off one by one.

Four of his men, though, Chavez, Wickman, Jules, and Jones calmly pick their shots.

"You have your orders, Johnson. Get on 'em," Riley says and hurries to the four picking their shots.

Wickman glances at him. "Think ya need a better class of Marines, Lieutenant."

"They're facing something that isn't supposed to exist," Chavez says. "Give 'em a break, Wick."

"Any of you see it?" Riley asks.

Jones shakes his head. "Moves too damn fast. I get it in my sights and it's gone before I can pull the trigger. It's big, though. All black."

"Silver eyes," Jules says.

"Yeah," Wickman says. "Freaky bastard."

"Has tentacles, I think," Chavez says.

Indeed, Riley thinks as he watches his men being yanked into the dark woods.

"Grenades," Riley says. "Throw them at different intervals in different areas."

They look at him like he's some exotic bird for a moment, then nod in unison. They unclip their grenades. Riley does the same.

He pulls the pin.

24

Kris leads them back towards Riley's operation when five explosions shake the ground and light up the horizon momentarily.

"Holy shit." Mel steps beside Kris.

"Guess the area isn't very secure anymore," Kris says.

Men begin to scream.

Gunfire crackles the night.

Kris says, "I gotta check on them."

"Or we can get to the vehicle and haul ass out of here," Mel counters. "Sounds like they have plenty of firepower."

"They might be our only way out, though," Kris says. She listens to them scream and to the sounds of M4s and pistols and SAWs chatter and crack.

"Sounds like they're having trouble," Mel says. "Will you listen this time, please? Let's get to the vehicle and leave."

"Mom." Tanner takes her hand. "Please?" He's almost as tall as she is, but she still thinks of him as her baby boy.

She squeezes his hand, and through the night vision goggles sees him smile. "Okay."

Kris turns in the direction of the Explorer, spares a glance at the gun blasts, listens to the screaming, and stops.

She grabs Tanner by the shoulders and turns him to face her. "Go with Mel. It's not far. I'll meet you there."

"*What*? Why?"

"Because they might need help, and I'm a soldier."

In the green goblin glow of the night vision, she watches a tear trickle down his face. Still, he nods. A firm nod. She hugs him tight.

When they part, Mel says, "You need to come with us. This is suicide."

"*Suicide*?" Tanner's voice cracks.

“Shh, honey,” Kris says to him. To Mel, she says, “Remember Afghanistan? Remember what you told us before we went into the shit storm?”

“Kris, that’s not—”

“You said, ‘It doesn’t matter if they’re Army or Marines, or Navy, or Airforce. If they’re ours, we do everything in our power to help those in dire situations.’ Well, basically like that.”

Mel rolls her eyes. “This is different. And you know it.”

“There are *Marines* in a dire situation, Captain.”

Mel’s lips press together. She turns away. “You’re putting all of us in danger, soldier. What about Tanner?”

“I understand, though,” Tanner says.

Everyone looks at him, then at Kris. Even Mel.

Finally, Mel sighs and says, “In and out. If you’re not at the vehicle in twenty, we’ll leave without you. Got it?”

“Yes, ma’am,” Kris says. She gives Tanner a hug, hesitates, then hands him the Smith and Wesson .45 pistol. “Your dad wanted to give this to you on your sixteenth birthday.”

Crying, he nods and hugs her one last time.

She takes off the night vision goggles and tries handing them to Mel.

“What—uh, no,” Mel says. “Those things make me sick. Keep them. I’ll take your rifle, though.”

Kris hands it over, snugs the goggles back over her head. “Take care of him, please.”

Mel smiles the tiniest bit. “Of course. See you in twenty.”

She watches them go. She watches until their pale, greenish bodies are nothing but specks in the heavy woods.

Then she turns and runs toward Lieutenant Riley’s operation as the gunfire mellows to a few cracks in the night.

25

On its side, one of the high-density lamps flickers, strobing the scene before her. Kris flips up the goggles.

All the air leaks from her lungs in a single wisp out of her mouth.

Chchchchch. A young man, maybe in his early twenties, fires his M4 into the woods. He roars something too garbled to understand.

They're not all dead, Riley's team. But most are. Mutilated bodies litter the ground. Somewhere in all this mess, someone is crying.

She makes her way toward a table with a few computer screens set up, along with a satellite radio. Whoever was manning these gadgets is gone now.

Another young man joins the other. They take turns shooting at whatever is in the woods.

There are other men, injured men. Two or three, with terror scratches over their faces.

Kris checks the screens on the table. At first, she doesn't really comprehend what's going on. Thinks that it might be a glitch. Hell, probably is. Yet, the more she watches the bright, red figure flicker from one screen to the other, the more she begins to believe it's real.

Something came out of Brooke, she thinks. A cold chill snakes under her skin.

A hand falls on her shoulder. She twists around, ready to strike.

"At ease," Riley says.

Blood covers the entire right side of his face, clothes ripped in more than a few places. His dark hair is a blood-caked mess. His bloodshot eyes shift, as if looking for something.

Kris glances around, then asks, "What happened?"

"It's not like the others," he says.

One of the younger soldiers fires his gun, screams something about a score to settle.

"What do you mean?"

His eyes almost look haunted when he says, "It has tentacles. It…it…and Red Team never showed up. Can't reach 'em. Our coms are down. Berk…we're cut off."

Kris resists the urge to slap the man. Instead, she says, "You're a Marine. You're *trained* to deal with being cut off."

He nods. "This is…" He motions to the two young men and all the dead or injured. He returns his bloodshot gaze to her. "We're not trained to deal with *monsters*."

"Yes, you are," Kris says. "You take care of the human ones daily. And it's just one?"

Again, Riley nods. "It moves too fast. We can't kill it. We—"

A black rope snaps out of the darkness, wraps around Riley's neck, and coils so tight his eyes bulge out of their sockets.

No, she has time to think. *Not a rope but a…a tentacle.*

Then Riley is yanked into the woods. A few seconds later, his screams devour even those of the young men.

A low chittering sound, like a slowed-down recording of a cicada, floats out of the woods.

Kris backs away, bumping into the table with the screens on it. One of them falls to the ground by her feet. She lifts the M4, heart trip-hammering.

Narrow, silver eyes blink at her for a second, then disappear.

Not green eyes, but silver.

Something came out of Brooke.

She hurries around the table, trying to think of what to do.

Her gaze falls on the two young Marines as they shoot at nothing, amped by fear and adrenaline. She's seen this before many times. When it happens, approaching soldiers in this state is a death sentence. They're pretty much in KILL EVERYTHING mode.

So she remains where she is as one injured soldier says, "It hurts." Most of the skin on his face is missing. "Kill me. Please."

Kris turns away to find another Marine, this one trying to tie a tourniquet around the bleeding stump of his left leg with his belt.

He's growling, teeth clamped onto a stick to stave off the screaming. He doesn't seem to notice her.

She draws in a deep breath, exhales slowly, and goes to help the man. He growls at her over the stick in his mouth and swats her hands away.

"Let me help," she says, reaching for the belt.

He drops the belt and presses the muzzle of his pistol to her forehead. It's still warm.

Slowly, she lifts her arms and backs away.

He lowers the gun and returns his attention to the belt, blood-slicked hand slipping over the material.

At this very moment, she realizes she can't help any of them. They've all lost their minds tonight. Those still alive, anyway. Marines. The toughest of them. Jesus, what the hell is out there? What kind of monster can subdue an entire platoon of Marine Force Recons? A deep sorrow spreads from her core out to her fingertips. A tingling ache. She can't help them.

And Mel is waiting for her. How long has it been already? Shit.

Kris hurries to the edge of Riley's camp.

Something lashes out, whips her feet out from under her. She falls hard on her right elbow. The puncture wounds in her shoulders scream. She scrambles away from the spot, lifts her gun.

"*Hoo-rah, ugly*!" The two young Marines jump in front of her, spraying bullets.

This isn't going well.

Not at all.

***

It recognizes the woman, yet doesn't understand. This is one reason why it hasn't killed her yet.

The men shoot at nothing but trees, as they've all done.

None of them are suitable hosts. They lack a mother's strength.

But the woman…yes. She will do. This woman who is so familiar. Like a distant, foggy dream. Unsubstantial.

She'll provide the perfect vessel for offspring. This is what matters most. For it knows it cannot survive alone for long in the world. Nor does it wish to hide like the weak creature in the cave that thought she was its mother.

It has no mother.

Offspring will create a legion. A mass of protection. There are no plans to take over the world. Not yet. Maybe not ever. But it must breed. This is what its instincts tell it. Breed, and survive.

The men, they're shooting more trees. The woman is getting to her feet now, looking unsure. This it feels as well as sees.

A stray bullet grazes the side of its head, a hot slice through the skin. It sucks in a sharp breath. The pain is enough to spur it into action again.

It's done playing with the men, anyway.

***

"What do you mean they're not responding?" General Berk yanks his tie loose.

Private Silva says, "I've tried numerous times, sir. Last communication was from Private Johnson at twenty-one hundred hours. They were under attack, sir."

Berk waves this away. "I know all of that, Silva. And nothing from Red Team?"

"Nothing, sir."

Berk sighs. He stares at the thermal images as the monitoring room beeps and staff click away at their computers. "What the hell is going on out there?" he says mostly to himself. He shakes his head, thinking about the call from Lieutenant Riley an hour or so ago now. Riley mentioned a couple familiar names, Kristin Jensen and Melanie Hernandez. He knows them. They are leaders of their own platoon, but Army, and he rarely deals with Army recons. Marines are his position. Still…he knows these women for their bravery in Afghanistan.

He clears his throat. "Contact General Hoover, Silva. Have him call me. And send the order to assemble a seek-and-destroy platoon. We may need to also contact Admiral Cline."

Private Silva blinks. "Yes, sir. SEALs are getting involved?

Berk stares at the thermal images. “Gonna need all we can get.”

26

There's no time to run.

The creature drops from the trees behind the young Marines.

It's a hulking monster with the same slick black skin as the others, though it stands on dog-like hind legs. Small tentacles slither out of its skin, licking the air. Unlike the other things, this monster's back isn't quite as hunched.

Kris backs away, pointing the M4 at the thing, about to shoot, then it picks up one of the Marines. Its claw holds the man's head like a pro basketball player palms a ball. The young Marine, he's screaming, thrashing. He kicks at the creature, making contact but inflicting no damage. The other Marine starts to turn away, ready to run. On the creature's left shoulder, black skin splits and an inch-thick tentacle shoots out. It spins around the man's waist, tightens. He cries out as the appendage squeezes.

Eventually, the Marine slumps, his cries choked out. A runner of blood dribbles out of his gaping mouth to the ground. The tentacle unwraps itself and slithers back under the monster's skin.

Kris can't take anymore.

She squeezes the trigger.

Bullets cut into the creature's back. Black blood spurts into the air. A howl of pain erupts from the beast. It drops the Marine, who immediately runs into the woods screaming. He doesn't even take the MP5 with him

Tiny, needle-thin tendrils wriggle over the bullet holes and…

My God, she thinks. *It's healing itself.*

The tendrils stitch the holes shut.

A violent shiver quakes the creature as it faces her. If it's the thing that came out of Brooke, it grew *fast*.

The thing towers over her. A hulking mass of darkness and thin, lashing tentacles. Its feet are massive paws that dig into the dirt. Its claws, long, black, and sharp, clench and unclench. Its chest is a barrel attached to an otherwise narrow torso.

Kris's sight lifts to its misshapen head, a mongrelizing of a gorilla, wolf, and possibly a lion. Thin lips peel away from long, white teeth that glimmer in the ambiguous light.

Slanted, silver eyes shimmer.

A deep growl rumbles through its grinning teeth.

Kris's stomach quivers at the sound… A sound that plucks at her sinews and gnaws on her nerves.

For a full five seconds, she can't even move.

The skin in the center of its chest spreads and a tentacle slips out, making a wet slurping sound. It slithers through the air, then caresses the right side of her face. Its touch is almost scalding. A stink like rotten eggs radiates from it.

Kris, breathing in gasps, manages, "Wh-what are you?"

The creature's eyes widen a bit. Then it bends and hisses into her sweaty, bruised face.

"Brooke."

Kris blinks. Icy shivers scuttle along her skin like hundreds of tiny spiders.

The tentacle slowly licks down the rights side of her face to her jaw, following the line all the way to her chin. The heat of it is near to burning. Its long teeth click as the monster chuckles. The tentacle squirms over her skin, from one side of her jaw to the other. Slow. Intimate.

A small whine forms in Kris's throat.

Chchchchch.

"*Hoo-Rah, ugly*!"

The young Marine. The one who ran. He's back and…

The thing turns as the Marine pumps it full of bullets. Its entire body shakes, thread-like tendrils already stitching its wounds.

The Marine, he's roaring.

This is what madness sounds like.

She wastes no time, pulls an extra clip from a fallen soldier, another grenade, and sprints into the woods.

Behind her, the Marine's roars turn to screams.

***

It doesn't know the woman, but its host did. And its host is still a small part of it. Its host's name was Brooke. There are flickers of information, slivers of vague memories, but nothing that lingers too long.

It crouches over the dead man, rips out his still warm heart, and chomps into it like an apple. Its silver eyes drift, skimming over the dead.

With the group before this one, it had been ravenous. It didn't take its time with them like this group. That other group, as soon as they lowered themselves into the woods, it pounced on them. Devoured them. Had its fill.

The need to breed hadn't yet surfaced fully.

Not like now.

It thinks about planting its seed in a couple dead men, just to see if the offspring take, then rejects the idea. Instincts tell it the dead are also unsuitable.

It stands fully and looks off in the direction the woman had fled. It grins, knowing it'll find her no matter where she goes. It has her delicious scent.

It moves out of the light, and into the dark.

***

Berk hangs up the phone and rubs his graying temples. He wants a drink. A stiff one. Straight bourbon. But that'll have to wait. He uncaps a bottle of Tylenol and washes down two capsules with a heavy swig of water. It won't work as well as bourbon, but it's something.

He managed to talk to General Hoover of the US Army and Admiral Cline of the US Navy. Both were considerably hesitant to send any of their men here, and Berk doesn't blame them. He'd be hesitant, too. But, they saw the reports and the thermals he had Silva send via email. They knew both teams, Red and Blue, are now unresponsive. They had all the facts and eventually agreed to help.

All this communication, however, garnered the attention of the Secretary of the State, the man Berk just got done talking to. It's attention Berk doesn't want just yet.

Now Mr. Secretary thinks Earth is being invaded by damn aliens. And, although Berk hasn't ruled the possibility out, he believes there's something else going on here.

A team of SEALS are en route, and two special ops platoons are no more than ten miles away. They'll all meet here on base and he'll brief them all on the situation.

Then his phone rings, and everything changes.

27

She runs deeper into the woods, away from Mel and the kids.

Can't lead that thing to them. She just hopes Mel gets the kids to safety.

Not Brooke, she thinks. *That's not Brooke*.

Ah, but it came out of her.

Kris read an article in a magazine a while back about parasites. Sometimes they take on the traits of their hosts. Sometimes a part of their host stays with them. Not memories, exactly, but something like it. Of course, the article said the study was inconclusive and there's no hard evidence, but that's the theory.

The heat of the creature's tentacle still lingers on her jaw. Her heart tumbles over itself as the woods surrounding her are bathed in the green ambiance of night vision.

She doesn't know if it's following her or not, but the way it acted back there, it didn't seem like it wanted to hurt her.

If so, then what the hell does it want with her?

The very thought sends terror through her in noxious, icy waves as she runs.

She breaks through the brush into their old camp, and stops, breath stuck in her throat like a fishbone.

After a moment, she manages, "Oh. Oh my God."

About a dozen men, Marines, lay dead. Through night vision, they appear ghoulish, covered in a thin layer of moss. And Brooke's body…

Kris's stomach lurches. Saliva fills her mouth, practically drowning her before she swallows it down. These soldiers, they're worse than Riley's team. Some are nothing but heaps of bloody, soaked bones with bits of meat still clinging to them.

She stumbles out of camp, drops to her knees, and vomits. Hot tears stream her face. She sniffles, gags.

I can't kill it. If it can do that to two platoons of Marines…I can't…

Somewhere behind her, a stick snaps.

Kris lunges to her feet and runs. She passes the hollow where they first realized they weren't alone in the woods. It feels like a million years ago. She leaps over bushes, breaks through thin branches.

Besides all this, the woods are as silent as a tomb.

Then she skids to a stop, lungs burning, legs quivering. In the goblin glow of the night vision stands the cave where all of those things came from, a pale emptiness through the goggles.

In front of the cave lies the nest.

She moves toward it cautiously. But after a long, good look, it seems all the eggs have exploded.

Still, she's not going to risk that shit. No way. Instead, she skirts the rock piles all the way to the mouth of the cave. Here, she stops again. A rancid odor she can't quite place flows out of the opening. But that's all.

Did we really kill them all?

One sure as shit way to find out.

Kris steps into the cave.

***

For a while, it actually loses her scent.

More than once, it doubles back, tentacles licking, nostrils flaring. But there's no trace of the woman.

It returns to the camp with all its meals from earlier. Its host still lay undisturbed.

It chitters, cups her pale check in its claw. The host gave it life, so it does not hate her. In fact, she's the closest thing to a mother it has.

It's here, in this camp, where the scent is lost.

Frantic, it retraces the trail again until it comes to the dead tree. Then…nothing.

Eventually, it stalks the perimeter of the camp.

And that's when it finds the vomit…and her scent.

***

It takes a lot longer than Berk wants for all four teams to gather in the hanger. He just hopes the briefing remains brief and doesn't drag out. He hopes that all of this hasn't been in vain.

But things have definitely changed.

"You're all here for a very specific and time-sensitive mission," he says, garnering even the SEALs attention. "We have discovered a viable threat in Maker's Wood, about thirty miles from here. It has claimed the lives of two Force Recon platoons and we believe there are survivors still out there." He stops, thinking of the two women, Kristin and Melanie. Then continues. "At twenty-one hundred hours, we lost communication with Blue Team. Lieutenant Riley's final words were, 'We are under attack by something not human.'" Berk looks at them pointedly. "Not human. That's what you'll be up against out there. Over a year ago, a small blip popped up on out radar. Barely a second. The private in charge logged it in his books, but there was no record of it otherwise and was not investigated."

The four teams glance at each other. To Berk, they look both confused and amused. He doesn't blame them. But here's where things change.

"And now I'll turn it over to Dr. Elsa Baum, Interdimensional Research Director for NASA."

He catches dubious glances, and steps aside as Elsa, a short, richly bronzed woman in her late-forties moves to the front of the platform.

She clears her throat and stands ramrod straight. She doesn't say anything for a long moment. Seated behind the platform is Jack, Director of Homeland Security, and Ben Whittley, Secretary of the State.

"When Secretary of the State Benjamin Whittley called me about the issue in Maker's Woods," Elsa finally begins, "and shared thermal image recordings of two days' worth, I did a little digging of my own. He was concerned about an extraterrestrial invasion. But at the mention of an unexplained blip on General Berk's radar a year and four months ago, I had my doubts, for it is known extraterrestrials have advanced cloaking devices." She pauses, not looking for reactions, but to possibly prepare the right words for the rest of her briefing. "What I found in our files was that on the exact same day, same hour, of the blip here, we also recorded spiked readings from our ISL, Interdimensional Signal Locator. So we believe something slipped out of its own dimension and into ours at this point."

One of the SEALS raises his hand. Berk nods and the man stands. He salutes Berk and turns fully to Elsa.

"Chief Miles Riggs, Ma'am."

She barely smiles, nods.

Chief Riggs, hands clasped behind his back, says, "Pardon me for the interruption, but are we to seriously believe there's an interdimensional creature gallivanting out in some woods? How come there's no intel of other dimensions?" He sits.

Elsa nods again. "Thank you, Chief Riggs. I realize that interdimensional travel, the very thought of if other dimensions as a possibility, seems like so much science fiction." She paces slowly back and forth on the platform. "But I assure you, it is not. The first interdimensional being to pass into our world happened fifty years ago. Since then, NASA created the top-secret Interdimensional Research Department. Not even the president knew we existed until ten years ago when not one, but two being appeared in New York City. Fortunately, no one was injured and we neutralized the threats. There is one dimension, D-6, that borders ours the closest. We believe these being came from D-6. As we also believe the same beings are now in Maker's Woods. Those beings, once autopsied, were found to have semi-symbiotic blood. It attached itself to the body and feeds on it, grows strong, then moves on to a new host. There was a female and male. The female contained eggs in development within her womb."

Elsa pauses again, perhaps letting it all sink in. Berk sure as hell needed the tiny space of time when they spoke on the phone earlier. Elsa had already been on her way, only a few miles from base by that point.

"The thermal images, slight because these beings have very low body temperatures, match those from New York City. The eggs also contain a symbiotic fluid, though more vicious than the blood, borders more on parasitic. The eggs work like proximity mines and explode if motion is detected. We observed, through our experiments, that once this fluid touches a host, it finds a way inside. There, it takes only half an hour or less for incubation. A new transformation emerges, destroying its host in the process. What is born is neither like the host, nor like its mother, though DNA proves it to be both. An entirely different species we call Obsidious."

Berk sighs. This is running on way too long. He approaches her and whispers in her ear that this is very time sensitive. She nods, looking a bit unnerved. He can tell she's not one to be interrupted, nor one to be rushed. Still, lives are at stake here.

"In conclusion," Elsa says. "According to recent thermal images, there are only about six or seven of the lower heat signatures in the area. Scattered. And one very strong signature. We believe this is the hybrid, the one you should destroy first and bag for further analysis. It has an ability to heal itself, but if you keep shooting, you should break through its skin to the vitals. There are also normal human signatures. Five. Four all in one place just outside the woods and one near a cave and tunnel system in the heart of the woods. The other beings, not the Obsidious, must most be destroyed to cease any further procreation. Bag these as well and send them to our facility."

Elsa steps off the platform and leaves the hanger without another word, no doubt pissed off.

Berk says, "Your orders are to infiltrate the woods, locate and immediately extract the human signatures, and eliminate the threat. US Army Special Ops, your priority is to locate and extract the survivors. US Navy SEALS and Marine platoon, Seek and Destroy; you're to locate and eliminate the threats, focusing on the hybrid. Hit it with all you got, men. It took out Red and Blue teams in no more than an hour. It's fast. Very fast."

He turns his attention to the six Marine snipers standing aside from the rest. "Team Exterminate, your objective is to hunt and bag the remaining creatures scattered throughout the woods." They nod.

Berk gives them all a serious glare he hopes conveys the concern he feels for them all. "Be careful out there. All of you. This is an enemy you've never fought before, and not even Elsa knows how to destroy it. All that's known is it can heal itself. Hit hard and keep hitting until it's dead." He pauses, then adds, "Dismissed."

They hurry to the choppers as Berk remains on the platform, wondering why he feels like he just sent them all to their deaths.

28

The dead thing on the floor inside the cave is larger than the others, but not by much.

It might seem even bigger if its head was still attached.

Its blood is also eating the body. Crushing. Thick smacking sounds as it feeds. The smell is so bad she has to pull her shirt collar up over her mouth and nose.

Kris keeps a good distance away from it, not wanting the blood to come after her.

This is a good thirty yards into the cave.

Beyond is a tunnel.

She faces the cave's opening.

If it tracks her by scent, then maybe the stink of the dead thing will mask her smell. Even so, there's nowhere in the cave to hide if it decides to check it out. Yet, going into the tunnel will mean she'll be trapped. No room to maneuver.

The thought of setting traps crosses her mind, but does she even have enough time? Will traps be effective? This isn't a damn movie. Traps take time. She might be able to run a trip wire across the mouth of the cave, set to pull grenade pins. But…grenades have a little delay. Four point five seconds to be exact. If the monster rushes in, it might be too far away for the grenades to do any real damage. It will also probably trigger a cave-in, trapping them both inside.

Kris moves toward the opening and stops.

But if she's out there, it'll track her easier. It can also wear her out like it did with Riley's team. It will move around so much that she can't shoot it.

She turns back to the tunnel.

Maybe it leads to another part of the woods? If she can cut her scent trail off here, then perhaps there's a chance at escape.

That's if the tunnel goes anywhere.

There's really no other choice.

Kris enters the tunnel as the goggle's low-battery symbol begins to flash.

***

Once again, the scent is lost.

It licks the ground and moves through the nest. Anger sizzles through every part of it. It hates itself for not grabbing her earlier. If not for that man shooting it in the back…

If not for thinking her scent will be easy to track…

Soon enough, though, it picks up her intoxicating aroma and traces it toward the cave where its dead mother still lies. About eight feet from the cave's opening, the scent dies away in the stench of the false mother.

It blinks at the cave's opening.

Would the woman really go in there? It doesn't think so, and is about to circle around the cave to search or her scent, when a long beep echoes out of the dark, rocky mouth.

***

The beep is loud, bouncing off the ragged walls of the tunnel.

"Shit," she growls.

She forgot the goggles give off a warning beep when the battery is about to die. It's a feature that's supposed to be done away with, since in the field it gives away a soldier's position. So many have fallen because of that infernal beep.

Only a single, long beep, but still. It's a death sentence, really.

And if that creature is anywhere near the cave, though…

Her pale green viewer flickers.

She has about fifteen minutes of battery life left. Probably less.

She picks up the pace while she can still see. The last thing she wants is to make a torch. It'll be like a damn beacon in here. HEY LOOK AT ME, flickering glow of death.

The tunnel slants downward at a casual grade, so slight she's barely aware of it. The walls are rough, not hewn or cut.

It's an old, natural tunnel then. Unless the creatures did this, which is also a possibility.

The deeper she ventures, the more the air kisses her with icy lips. There are openings on the right side of the wall. Kind of like small crawl spaces. She imagines the creatures hibernating in these narrow spaces during winter, a whole family of beasts from God knows where.

She hasn't had much time to reflect on it, but she assumes they're aliens. Because, why not? Surely they're not from Earth. Or perhaps they are. Perhaps they once lived in this region millions of years ago, got buried or frozen deep underground. And with the climate changes, maybe…

Okay, that sounds just as rational as aliens. And aliens are still more believable. The Earth holds many secrets, she has no doubt, but these things…? For some reason, she just can't wrap her head around the idea.

And, hell, she could be totally wrong about it all.

But if Berk sent recon teams here, then something's definitely up. He saw a threat and acted on it, though he might have underestimated the threat's potential.

What if they're some kind of mutant bred in a biotech lab somewhere around here? she thinks.

That feels a little more realistic, but…

Kris quickens her pace, jogging through the tunnel, thinking, trying to figure out her next move.

She's so wrapped up in her thoughts that she sees the pit two seconds too late.

Kris digs her heels in, pinwheels her arms, arches backward, but to no avail. Her momentum carries her forward into the pit. A slight cry of surprise springs out of her.

Then she's falling.

***

It sniffs the dead false mother and watches the blood feed on the corpse. Soon, the blood will be strong enough to go out on its own to find a suitable host.

All well and good, but where's the source of the beep? Where's the woman?

It stares at the tunnel deeper into the cave for a long time. Something, a voice so small it barely notices, tells it that the woman wouldn't go into the tunnel. She wouldn't trap herself in like that. Too smart.

And it almost believes this tiny voice. Almost.

Then a very faint cry echoes from the tunnel.

Barely a sound.

But it's enough.

It moves toward the tunnel, grinning.

***

Ripping off a few fingernails, her right hand latches onto a small jut of stone.

Pain laces her hand. From the weight, more pain shoots up and down her arm. Blood from the scraped fingertips and missing nails dribbles under the cuff of her jacket and slicks the stone.

Grunting, Kris reaches up with her left hand, grabs another knob of stone, and pulls herself tight against the wall of the pit. The toes of her boots find purchase on the rough wall. A sob wrenches out of her. Hurt. Tired. Beaten. There's no way she can live through this.

Then end it now, a dark voice in her head whispers.

Kris's eyes lower. There's a bottom, but it's a good thirty or forty feet down. So, she can't, in fact, end it here. Can't just let go and fall to her doom. If she drops from this height, she'll either break both legs, back, or neck.

Well, that dark voice croons, *if you're paralyzed, you won't feel whatever it has planned for you, right*?

The horrible thing is…she almost believes this inner voice, the sound of her weakness. She almost gives in.

Yeah, she could let go and hope she breaks her neck or back, or—

I can climb back up and fight. Or…

I can climb down and find a way out.

Two choices to live, to at least fight for survival. Falling is the coward's way out.

Above, the pit is a greenish ring. It flickers as the goggles battery loses more and more juice. It'll either climb out and try to jump across the pit in order to get to the other side, or go back to the cave. Or climb down.

She's still trying to decide the best course of action when a low growl sounds from above.

Shit.

It makes the decision easier, though.

Kris climbs the rest of the way down. The bottom of the pit is soft and sandy. It only takes a few seconds to realize it's not just a pit, but a hole to yet another tunnel. It leads in both directions. Still, she chooses the direction she was going above. Straight forward. She hurries to get out of sight in case the monster looks into the hole.

Moving as quietly as she can, the night vision goggles flicker crazily, then go out.

And darkness consumes her.

***

It leaps across the pit, but her scent isn't on this side.

So where…?

It steps to the edge of the pit and peers down.

A stronger odor mingles with her scent… Blood.

It crawls down the side of the pit, stomach gurgling from the blood.

29

Scratching noises fill the void of black as Kris shuffles along, arms outstretched, fingers slipping over rough stone.

What the hell was she thinking? She should have known the goggle's battery would die sooner rather than later.

If she'd went back outside, maybe she could have found a way to fight the thing, or lose it long enough to figure out a decent plan.

The ground rises, slanting upward a bit.

The only sounds are of her shaky breathing and the slight scratching noises behind her.

Something is in the dark with her. Something creeping closer…closer.

She feels around on the belt the medic gave her for a knife. She needs to have some form of light. She needs to know where…

Kris doesn't find a knife, but something better. Heart pounding, she pulls a small flashlight out of its pouch.

Behind her, not far, something growls, thick and rumbling. It's a sound that shudders along the ragged walls to her fingertips, shivering up her arm, and finally quaking her heart. Blood crashes in her temples. Her skin lumps like chicken skin.

Closer still, she hears a slight chittering sound.

It's right behind her, closing in. Soon, she'll feel hot, deadly tentacles slip around her neck. Soon…

"So tasty," it whispers.

Hot breath puffs on the back of her neck, ruffling her ponytail. In the complete darkness, Kris's eyes widen.

Slowly, she unstraps the M4.

"What do you want?" she asks the thing.

Very close to her left ear, it says, "You."

An icy shiver shakes through her. Something hot and slimy slithers along the nape of her neck.

Kris screams, spins, and pulls the trigger. Gunfire sputters light in the tunnel. In this strobing light, the monster reels backward, arms and claws swatting at bullets like they're killer bees. She keeps shooting, moving forward as it stumbles back. Her scream changes into a roar. Black blood spurts and mists. It splashes the walls of the tunnel. Gunsmoke chokes her, but she doesn't stop shooting.

The monster shrieks, drops to its knees.

In the fluttering flashes, Kris watches black skin slough off and splat onto the ground. It shrivels away from an ashen underlayer.

It has two layers of skin?

With this revelation, she aims at the ghostly patch in the center of the thing's chest. Blood the color of pea soup sprays.

Six shots and—

Clickclick. Darkness envelopes them.

The mag is empty.

In the dark, the creature grunts. A shuddery mewl finds her ears.

Kris ejects the spent mag and slaps a fresh one in. She's about to pummel the monster with more rounds when—

"This is the US Navy SEALS! Is anyone down there?"

Kris sucks in a gulp of cordite and coughs.

She's about to answer the man, then something smacks the side of her head. Hard.

And she knows no more.

***

More of those men!

It watches the woman fall to the ground and stands. Pain stabs through its chest. If she had continued…

"US Navy SEAL here," the man shouts from above. "We have pinpointed your location. Are you injured?"

Rage rips through the pain.

It waits a moment, allowing it skin to heal, then rushes to the bottom of the pit.

The woman will have to wait.

***

The screaming pulls her out of unconsciousness, though she's not fully aware of this at first because, *pitch black*. Then gunshots ring down the pit into the tunnel.

Kris, head throbbing, finds the flashlight on the sandy ground and turns it on.

The creature is gone. Its black skin and blood writhes a few feet from her, searching for anything to latch onto.

Slowly, she stands, hand on the wall as her balance steadies. The pain in her head, it's like a bunch of rubber mallets thumping her repeatedly. The entire right side of her face burns.

It must have hit her with one of its tentacles.

And what about the Navy SEAL who called out?

The screaming. The gunshots. It's all coming from above. It's not loud enough to be in this tunnel, more echoes than anything. Far away noises that really aren't that far away.

Alright, cool. Fine. You figured it out. Now move your ass!

Kris faces away from the hole leading topside and, at first, can't move more than a fast walk. But, gradually, her pace quickens to a jog. The gunshots float farther behind. She keeps the small LED flashlight pointed ahead as the ground continues to slant upward.

Everything hurts and the incline doesn't help at all. Her legs burn. Her lungs are proverbial sacks of lava. Her arms feel like thirty-pound bags of sand attached to her shoulders. And her head…ugh. Yet, she can't stop. The more distance put between her and that monster, the better.

But still, more help is here. This time, it's the SEALS, which are just as badass as Marines. Hopefully, Berk sent more than two teams this time, though. If not, SEALS or no SEALS, that thing will decimate them.

Unless they figure out what she did. Unless they find that ashen second layer of skin.

And she's still not sure if that means anything.

Still, maybe the black stuff is like armor? Destroy the armor, kill the monster.

And if the soldier hadn't distracted her…if she'd just kept shooting it, then maybe…

No time to dwell on what could have been.

Her jog becomes a run, and soon the incline evens out a bit, though the ceiling is lower and spiked with small stalagmites. The air, it grows even colder and damp. The kind of air that really chomps into a person like frigid teeth.

Before long, she's moving in a low crouch. Then she's on her hands and knees, slogging through thick, chilly mud.

If there's an end to the tunnel, she doesn't see it. Though the mud indicates something, right? That maybe water is getting down here through somewhere?

Yes.

But that somewhere might be a six-inch hole for all she knows.

Still, gotta keep moving.

Hope dwindles, however, with every second.

***

These men…they're smarter than the others. Faster. They keep moving around and never stop shooting.

It managed to kill three of them before they regrouped and attacked.

Its skin, in some places, droops off its body, exposing its much more fragile flesh beneath. These spots it tries to keep hidden and it tries to move faster than the men.

That woman, though. That awful woman. She really injured it down in the tunnel. Its movements are slower. Every lunge or attempt at attack is a geyser of agony throughout its chest.

It tries to focus the pain into more rage, fuel its movements, but these men are relentless. Their aim is too true.

It crawls up the side of the cave, drops down onto one of the men, and rips his head from his body. It throws the head at another man, but he just steps aside and keeps shooting, unfazed.

Now the pain is nearly unbearable as more bullets find their way through the outer skin.

And they don't stop shooting.

It squeals, lashing tentacles out wildly. One of these smacks the gun out of a man's hand, while another impales him.

There are six men left.

But if it stays here, it'll surely die.

No matter how much rage rampages through it.

So it does what it has to do.

It crawls to the top of the cave and out the opening like a spider, leaving long smears and pools of pale green blood in its wake.

***

Tepid, though fresh, air wafts into her sweaty face and all Kris can do is lie in the cold mud, letting it soothe her throbbing head.

She'd been through hell and back before. She was lost in the horrid sewers of Saudi Arabia for two days, captured in North Korea and tortured until Brooke and Mel rescued her, survived the nasty jungles of Vietnam on an intel search-and-destroy mission.

But this…

She's never felt so damaged in mind, body, and spirit, so beaten to the point of giving up. It's a rocky, sharp edge she teeters on this very moment as she lies in the mud, half in and half out of the tunnel. Tears trickle down her bruised cheeks.

What if it's crawling up behind you right now? the dark inner weakness whispers.

Kris, a whine rising in her throat, kicks herself out of the tunnel and into a drift of leaves. They crunch and crackle under her as she sinks into them.

Eyes shut, she breathes in the musty dankness.

A familiar mewling sound sifts through the leaves to her ear.

Kris's eyes pop open. The air in her lung gushes out. The mewling, it's getting closer… so close that the thing has to be pretty much standing over her.

She doesn't move. Can't breathe. Her heart ka-thuds so hard that blood whooshes in her ears. Her guts are a twisted mess, squirming around like fat worms.

Right next to her, she hears the crackling of leaves, the throaty mewling. Right next to her, the monster stands. Does it know she's here? Can it smell her?

A few seconds pass, and she wonders if maybe it's toying with her now. Maybe it's playing a sick game or pretending that it doesn't know where she is and is waiting for her to pop up out of the leaves and try to run. And, oh, ha-ha, what a fun game we're playing, right, Kris? Here, let me twist your head off and slurp on the fount of blood that sprays out your neck.

Kris shakes her head, throat working, saliva filling her mouth. She's going to puke. She's going to puke and that will be that. Because if it doesn't know where she is now, if she tosses chunks, it'll definitely know.

Then, heavy footfalls and crackling leaves move away from her.

Might be a trick, though. Distant, the monster mewls again.

Somewhere, not far, someone shouts, "Chief, we have a blood trail!"

"Ramirez, Brown, Connolly," says a deeper voice. "You stay with me. It might double back. Carter and Daniels, track it. Follow and report, but do not engage. I repeat, do *not* engage."

Quick thumps of boots hurry by her.

Move, she tells herself. *You gotta move*.

Kris crawls out of the leaves, groaning. Let the SEALS handle the monster. She needs to get out of here and get to a hospital or something. She takes a moment to find her bearings, and when she does, she runs in the direction of the Explorer.

If Mel made good on her promise, then they should already be gone. Which is good. She'll just follow the road out and into town and meet up with them there. It's only about ten miles. She can make it.

Minutes fly by without her being aware. She's too focused on getting to the road and getting the hell out of here. She's had enough.

On her right, the sound of Plains Waterfall. Getting closer now.

Not too much longer.

She almost believes she'll make it out alive, then she hears the mewling.

30

It consumes the last of the mother it once flowed through, except the teeth. The teeth are too difficult to absorb, so they lay scattered in the flaky remains of the mother.

It slithers through the deepest shadows, slipping out of the cave unnoticed.

It has fed well and now it needs a home, a place where the elements won't be so harsh on its being.

Around it, creatures stomp and yell as they run in every direction. Its vision is such to where these things are nothing but hulking blurs. The ground, though, trembles with their passing. The air has an electric buzz which tingles all the way to its center. There's a weight to it. And, oh, all the tastes. It remains in the shadows, tasting the thickness of the air, the creatures' sweat and energy. So *alive* these things are. So perfect.

The stuff that used to run as blood through the mother winds around a small tree until it's safely hidden, yet sense the creatures clearly scurrying below. It oozes over a branch…and waits.

***

The mewling turns out to be a cat. Something is wrong with its left hind leg. It might not be broken, but hurt pretty bad. It limps out of some heavy brush when Kris stops, thinking it's the monster.

Kris blows out a long breath that's not quite a sigh. Sporadic gunshots scatter the night air, echoing through the trees.

The cat winds itself around Kris's legs, purring and mewling. Every once in a while, it falls because of the bad leg.

Under much different circumstances, she might consider taking the poor thing with her. Maybe taking it to a vet or shelter. Or, hell, even keeping it for a pet and nursing it back to health. But she has to get to the road. She has to make sure Tanner is okay. If she dies out here, he'll be alone. No mother. No father. Sure, Mel might fight to adopt him, but God only knows how much she'll have to fight. Both of Kris's parents are gone. Kyle's dad is still kicking, barely, though currently stuck in a wheelchair, breathing through an oxygen mask.

The man hadn't smoked a day in his life, yet somehow got lung cancer. The world works in mysterious ways alright.

Kris leaves the cat mewling behind her. Her heart aches a bit, and if they make it out of this, she'll come back for it. That's if it's still in the area. With the hurt leg, she doesn't imagine it'll travel far.

She jumps across the narrow ravine, sucking a sharp breath in through clamped teeth from the mound of pain that's her body. Everything hurts. Even her damn hair.

Still, she can't afford to stop anymore. She has to keep moving. The more ground she puts between the monster and her, the better. She hopes the SEALS smoke the sucker.

Flashlight beam bouncing, she runs as fast as her weary body will let her, which isn't much more than a brisk jog. Her legs feel like pillars of gelatin. Everything about her head is a throbbing, miserable blob. Even so, she's on a mission. The sole objective: Getting the hell out of Maker's Woods.

It soon becomes her mantra. GET OUT GET OUT GET OUT.

But she can't hear Plains Waterfall anymore, and suddenly, she doesn't know where she is. The waterfall has always been an indication that you're close to the road. You only have about ten more minutes and you're out of the thick stuff and on your happy, jolly way back to civilization where there's always light and walls between you and whatever might be stalking the night.

Kris stops, swinging the flashlight back and forth. There should be a trail here and broken limbs, tromped-down weeds, signs of passage from when she broke the trail. Yet there's nothing here but heavy brush and to her right a huge patch of hawthorn trees, all of them sporting their long, sharp thorns.

The way is definitely not through those.

She can't even remember seeing hawthorn trees on their way to their soon to be camp.

So…where the shit am I?

And how? She knew she was going the right way. The waterfall told her that much. Then again, her head is mush, inside and out. Did she black out for a moment? Just long enough to veer off course? Like sleep jogging, or something?

The problem stirs a stew of anxiety in her stomach. She's never done something like this before.

Kris turns in a slow circle, flashlight beam crawling over trees and brambles and high weeds and—

Silver eyes blink.

The beam jerks to a stop. Kris pulls in a slow breath and slowly moves the beam back. Six inches. A foot. Two—

Black lips wrinkle away from long, pointed teeth.

"Oh shi—"

The monster bursts out of the high weeds, its high-pitched squeal breaking the air. It leaps. Kris doesn't even have time to lift the M4. The beast slams into her like one of those giant NFL linemen. The next thing she knows, she's on the ground, gasping for air and clawing for the M4. It slaps the gun out of her hands, spraying a few rounds wildly into the air. A tentacle wraps around her left wrist and yanks her to her feet.

Kris struggles with the tentacle. She hooks a couple fingers between it and her wrist. And the appendage tightens down more, pinning her fingers in place. She growls and thrashes. She kicks at the creature.

It lifts her higher. Face to face, those long, sharp teeth are no more than an inch from her nose. Silvery drool leaks around the corners of its hideous grin. Its breath smells like a bucket of dead leeches left out in the sun for a day or two. Her stomach lurches. She quickly swallows down a lump in her throat.

She hears the chattering of gunfire. The monster's body shakes. It screams, rearing, its huge maw wide open.

The tentacle releases her wrist and she falls to the ground. Then someone is helping her up, shouting, "Gogogogo!"

It's one of the SEALs. He's pulling her away from the creature as another blasts the monster full of bullets. In the beam of the light fixed to his MP5, pale green blood sprays in every direction.

"Wait," she says and dashes back to grab her flashlight.

Then the SEAL is pulling on her again. He says, "I'm Petty Officer Douglas." They plunge through a thicket of brambles. "We're here to rescue you." They jump over the ravine, running faster, her body screaming. "Do you know where the others are?"

"Oth-ers?" she pants.

"In your group. Do you know—?"

A black blur crashes into Officer Douglas like a high-speed locomotive. He flies through the air, smacks into the trunk of a large oak and crumples to the ground face first. He's not moving.

Tentacles whip around Kris's waist and squeeze. The monster looms over her, its entire body shifting and shuddering. A deep, bubbly growl works its way up the creature's thick throat. Its silver eyes narrow to slits.

"Hey," Petty Officer Douglas says. "If you're gonna kill someone, better make sure they're dead."

Those silver eyes widen. It whirls, tentacles slackening around Kris. Then they tighten again. She's lifted off the ground and swung over to the monster's right side.

Douglas remains emotionless. He has the MP5 pointed at the creature. A thin trickle of blood runs down the side of his face. "Put her down."

The beast lets out a jagged chuckle and slowly shakes its misshapen head.

Kris can tell by the slight slackening of Douglas's face that he didn't expect the creature to be intelligent. Or at least as responsive.

"Put her down," Douglas repeats.

Again, the creature shakes its head.

Kris jams the muzzle of the M4 into the side of the monster's head and fires. The tentacles release her. She starts toward Douglas when he shakes his head. He nods at the woods behind her. Then his calm eyes return to the creature.

"Alright, ugly," he says. "Let's do this shit."

Black skin stitches itself together along the side of its head as it straightens and faces Douglas. He fires a few rounds at it. It moves toward him. He shoots it again. It moves closer.

Then he unloads on the creature. The MP5 chatters, spurting tiny flickers of fire from the muzzle. The beast shrieks and swats at the bullets as it has before. It backs away.

"Go," Douglas roars over the chattering gun.

Kris hesitates. She's a soldier. She should help him. Should move beside him and shoot the thing in the same spot like before, and when the ashen under-layer is revealed, keep shooting. Why run and have to face the thing again when—?

"Mom!" She barely hears it over the gunfire, but…

She blinks and draws in a shuddery breath. Kris turns around, eyes searching the dark. Surely it's just—

"Mom! Help!"

"Tanner," she whispers and sprints into the woods, flashlight cutting through the night.

***

As it tries to fend off the man shooting it—tries to escape but every bullet is such a paralyzing, searing heat—it wonders if maybe it shouldn't just forget about the woman and seek an easier host.

Ah, but things have progressed beyond mere breeding now, haven't they? Oh yes. Because all a host really needs to be is alive to carry offspring. At least that's what its instincts tell it. For all the trouble she's caused, it feels like punishing her trumps breeding right now. How delicious it'll be when it rips the arms from her body. How it'll make her watch as it feeds on her, bit by bit. And if she dies, then it'll seek a better host. Either way, she needs to pay for all the pain she's caused it.

But first, it needs to deal with this man.

It leaps to the side. Bullets spray the air around it. The man shouts something it doesn't understand. Sometimes it understands them; sometimes not. It blames its host for this. It'd rather not understand. It hates their tones of their voices.

It races around the man, pushing itself faster than it should with all the pain it's in. Doing what it needs to do. Because—

The man spins, taking it off guard, and slams a fist into its stomach. It sends its tentacles to wrap around his arm and body. The punch was nothing.

Then the man begins to laugh. A full, throaty laugh.

It cocks its head, not understanding. He should be in pain from the squeeze of the tentacles. He should be trying to escape. Instead, he's laughing.

He says, "Y-you're not as smart as you think you are, ugly." He glances down.

It follows the glance. Still not understanding. Still not…

Then it sees. The man pulls his arm back as far as the tentacles will allow. And it sees in the man's hand, between him and it, is an oblong object. Its eyes widen, return to the man.

He grins and says, "Boom, motherfucker."

***

"Mom! Help!"

Her heart whip-cracks against the walls of her chest to the sound of her son's voice. It's definitely Tanner. Her boy. But how? Mel should've gotten them all out long before now. They should be in town. Safe.

She runs, legs screaming at her to stop. But she can't stop. She won't. Her baby is out there and he needs her. Something must have happened on the way to the—

An explosion broke the night.

Kris skids to a stop and turns in the direction she came. All she sees through the trees is a distant spray of sparks, or embers. Still, she knows what a grenade sounds like.

And that had definitely been a grenade.

Good, she thinks, turning away. *Hopefully, it blew that bastard apart*.

But if the grenade didn't hit one of the exposed places…

She shakes her head. No time to think about it right now. Kris swings in the direction she last heard Tanner calling from. South? Yes. Southwest, maybe. She waits, listing. Hoping. But he never calls out again.

A horrid sinking in her chest plummets to her stomach. She wipes tears off her face before she even realizes she's crying.

Kris swings the flashlight back and forth.

Somewhere deeper in the woods, a couple of gunshots sound, distant pops that reverberate amongst the trees.

She doesn't know what to do. Needs some sort of direction. Needs…

The men creep out of the foliage in the glow of her flashlight, and she almost shoots them.

"At ease, Sergeant," a familiar, stout man says. He holds up a hand. "They didn't tell us it'd be you we're here to rescue."

She knows the face, round and heavily whiskered. Knows the voice, deep and rough. But his name eludes her. Still, she lowers the M4.

He looks around and hurries to her. "Captain Shawn Bell. We met briefly in Afghanistan. Operation Drift, if you remember."

Finally, it all clicks together in her brain. Of course she remembers Operation Drift. It's what made her small team famous. Well, not famous, but highly respected. They infiltrated an enemy base, destroyed the coms, and collected vital intel. But it was what happened sneaking out of the base that got them the respect.

They were almost to the perimeter, almost home free. Then two dust-caked Jeeps rolled up the gates. Kris, on a whim, decided to check them out through a pair of binoculars. And sitting in the passenger seat of the first Jeep was one of the most wanted Taliban leaders. She whispered to Mel who was in the passenger seat, and Mel made the call to add one final objective. Capture the man and bring him back to their base, which was little more than a few flappy tents and a couple latrines. That was the new objective.

But they weren't prepared for seize, capture, and transport. There were only six of them. They were formed as a solitary Special Ops team, solely used for infiltration and intel collections, and sometimes for assassinations. Kris tried to get Mel to go the easier assassination route with the guy. Just bang, he's dead, now skedaddle. But both Mel and Brooke agreed that the man might hold extremely valuable intel. He needed to be brought in for interrogation.

And they did. They managed to kill the guards and his escorts. They stole one of the Jeeps and drove to the base. An hour later, a transport arrived to carry the man away for questioning. Kris was later told that the man took a day to break, and he spilled everything. He gave up intel that no doubt led to more successful missions thereafter.

Captain Bell had been the transportation team that took the man away.

Now, he's here to take her away, here to rescue her. But…

"Have you run into Captain Melanie Hernandez?"

Bell shakes his head. "You're the only heat sig we've found."

Tears well in her eyes, blurring her vision. "Did…did you find an Explorer?"

Again, he shakes his head. "No."

She's not even sure if this should give her relief or not.

Bell says, "Come on. We're getting you out of here."

But she pushes him away. "No. My son. Tanner. I have to find him. One of those things got him. He's stuck to a tree somewhere and I gotta find him."

"I'm afraid I can't let you do that, Sergeant."

"Like hell you can't. Give me couple M4 mags and I'll—"

"On our six, Cap," a young man says behind Bell. He's holding up a small monitor. "Strong heat sig. Moving slow."

"Shit," Bell says and looks Kris hard in the eyes. "That thing, it's a hybrid. Very hard to kill."

"Yeah." She almost laughs. "I kinda figured that out already."

"You have to hit it with all you've got—"

"In the same place and the black skin will either fall off or peel away. Underneath is another layer. Pale. Gross looking. That's how you kill it."

He blinks at her, totally shocked.

She knuckles away tears, smiles, chuckles. "Told you I kinda figured it out already."

"We didn't know about the other layer, though," Bell says.

"Now you do."

"Cap," the soldier holding the small screen says. "On our two. It's circling, sir."

Captain Bell spins a finger in the air and his men ready themselves.

"You can't all fire in the same place," Kris says. "It'll move around a lot. That's why the other teams died. They kept trying to follow it, and by the time they get a lock on it, it was somewhere else."

Bell nods. "Thank you, Sergeant." He hands her another M4 mag. "Might need your help."

She slips the mag into the empty slot on the medic's belt and asks for a grenade as well. He gives her one without question.

"Right flank, Cap," the young man says. "Circling slow. Bright red heat sig."

"Have four of your men follow it and the others wait," Kris says. "When it moves, we'll have a better range to work with."

Bell says, "Thank you, Sergeant." He gives his men the orders.

Then…they wait.

***

Its skin hangs in lifeless strings on its body. Its limp tentacles drag through the dirt behind it like black intestines. It sucks in a gargling breath, lurches, always keeping an eye on the men to its left.

They know it's here. The tension in the air gives them away.

The grenade (somehow it knows what the thing was called) had blown the man to pieces, and might have done more damage to it if it hadn't shoved the man back at the last second. Not fast enough, though. The grenade's shrapnel, the very explosion of the thing, killed most of its outer skin layer, it's protection. Agony slices through it. Not just in spots now, but everywhere.

From the corner of its eye, through the skim of trees, it fixes its attention on the woman.

It can't wait to feast off her insides.

***

The four Special Ops men follow the heat sig, tracking it in a rudimentary U-shape.

A stick snaps, but otherwise, the woods are quiet.

Kris keeps her M4 ready. Tired eyes scan the scene. Her face feels super swollen; probably the bruises. But she imagines the crying is making it even worse, especially around her eyes.

One thing is certain: Tanner yelled for her. If Mel made it out with them, he wouldn't be yelling. So he's here. In the woods. And even if he somehow escaped one of those things, he's out there all alone, wandering aimlessly through the woods at night, which makes it ten times worse… With or without the monsters.

The rest of Bell's team remain on full alert. Not frantic and blood hungry, but cool and calm. Ready for anything. Ready for—

"It's mov—"

Kris is knocked off her feet. She lands hard on her back. All the air shoots out of her lungs. She opens her mouth, trying desperately to breathe.

Bell shouts, "Fire!" *Chchchchch.* All around her, guns spit bullets.

Slowly, she's able to breathe again. Kris sits and rolls away before getting stomped on by the creature.

And for a moment, she can't move. The creature's black skin, what's left of it, dangles in drippy tatters like an old wet shawl on its hulking frame. Its tentacles lie limp in the dirt. The entire front of its torso is ashen and smeared with pale green blood. Blood that mists through crisscrossing flashlight beams.

It shrieks, this thing that should not be, this unknown abomination. It screams at the soldiers as they pump bullets into it.

Kris stands, backs away, and that's when she hears her son shout, "Mom! Please help!"

All of her nerves snap at the sound. A sizzling intensity zaps along her spine.

She doesn't even look back when she leaves.

Her baby needs her.

31

All it knows is agony. All it feels is pain after pain, after pain. An endless torture.

Is this how men really are? Kill something because it wants to live?

That woman. This is all her fault.

It goes to rip her head off, even as the men blast it full of more holes, but she's gone.

She's not anywhere around it. It roars in the hottest anger any creature has ever felt. And in its anger no longer feels pain. Something inside changes. Shifts.

From out of the bullet holes, new tentacles shoot out. They take out the closest of the men.

There's another shift inside it. This one painful.

It doubles over, too hurt, too scared to even scream.

Something is happening and it doesn't know what. A change it feels, yet cannot fathom. A force it can't control.

The men, they've stopped shooting. They're all staring.

And now, the shifting pain within eases. It straightens, mewls, because exhaustion from the agony and anger has drained most of its energy.

They look at each other. It and the men, really, for the first time, an understanding passes between them. It has a brief moment of respect for them. A moment of hope.

Then the thing within bursts out of its back.

***

The shooting stops, but she doesn't care. Maybe the monster is finally dead. Good.

Soon, she finds herself standing at Ghost Rock. She turns, looking for her boy.

"Tanner," she shouts, not caring who or what hears her.

She waits a few seconds and calls his name again.

Nothing.

Rage, white and hot, burns through her. She kicks the old boulder. She screams, because the anger is just too great to contain. Eventually, the screams change to heavy sobs. She crumbles to the ground and for the first time wonders if this is how madness sets in. Soon, she won't even know she's crazy.

God, she's so stupid. Why'd she even think it was a good idea to come here, let alone stay after that thing took the turkeys? What kind of mother *does* that? Brooke knew what they needed to do. She knew they had to leave. And if Kris had just listened, if she hadn't been so stubborn, maybe none of this would be happening.

"Mom! Help!"

Kris lifts her head, wipes away tears, and points the flashlight in the direction the voice came from, which is back toward the monster and Captain Bell's team.

She struggles to her feet. "Stay where you are, honey!"

Faint, but there, "Okay."

No. Not crazy. That's really Tanner!

Kris rushes back toward Captain Bell's team. She shouts, "Keep talking, kiddo!"

But he doesn't.

She opens her mouth to call out again when something bursts through the brush and runs into her. They both go down. Another second or two, and she realizes it's a soldier. He scrambles away from her, breathing heavily.

Kris points the flashlight at him, and grimaces. The soldier's face is littered with small cuts. She vaguely recognizes him as one of Bell's team.

Eyes wide, wild, he says, "Run. You gotta run. It's…it's…"

"What?" she asks. "You didn't kill it?"

He tries to go around her, but she catches his arms and swings him around.

"Easy," she says. "What's going on?"

"It…something came *out* of it. Tore through us like we—like we were nothing. So *fast*…"

"What…?"

"Run," he says to her. "We shot it and it *still* kept coming."

He wrenches out of her grip and sprints away. She lets him go, trying to wrap her head around what he told her.

Something else came out of the monster?

Jesus, this is like an endless nightmare… Only the nightmare is real and it'll eat you.

"Help me, Mom! Help!"

Tanner's voice is more distant now. It's hard to tell which direction, though. Maybe he had to move. Maybe this new monster is after him now?

The very thought ices her blood. He has his pistol, but if it took out Bell's team…

She moves out, a bit more cautiously now. There's a new threat out there, and the last thing she wants is to be caught off guard.

Okay, so maybe she isn't going crazy. If she wasn't a trained soldier, though, able to handle things differently than your average person, she'd be talking to the trees and making a skirt out of dead leaves by now.

"Tanner?"

She keeps moving. Tanner doesn't answer.

The air is different, too. Not thicker, nor thinner. But, there's this palpable heaviness to it. It's a sense that things have gone from horrible to worse in just a few minutes, an almost claustrophobic intensity she can't deny. Indeed, it's like the trees are closing in around her, like the bushes are creeping closer, and before long, they'll get her.

Her flashlight beam lands on the twisted remains of Captain Bell. Literally twisted, like an obscure pretzel. His arms and legs are broken. Sharp shards of bone poke out through his clothes. His face is eternally frozen in a silent scream.

Kris takes the light attached to his M4 and fixes it to hers. She put the small flashlight back in its pouch on her belt.

Scattered behind Bell are the rest of his team. All dead, all twisted husks.

Kris manages a weak breath and moves around the dead. She keeps her movements slow, scanning the dark with the light attached to her M4. Thick smacking sounds find her ears. She steps closer, moves the light over a few bodies, across a strand of saplings, and—

It crawls on top of one of the corpses. Long, gangly arms hook around the body and its claws dig deep. Its protruding jaws open, revealing rows of small, pointy teeth. Black eyes stare at her with emotional indifference. Along both flanks of its gaunt body slither dozens of tentacles. In the LED light, its skin shimmers an oddly alluring blue.

For a long moment, neither of them moves.

It's maybe the size of a Rottweiler, though not nearly as broad. It blows out a long, chittering noise.

Kris says, "Don't you things ever fucking die?"

It flinches, as if she threw a rock at it or something. Its claws rip out of the body and it creeps toward her, all those tentacles thrashing.

Kris opens fire, aiming for its head.

The creature takes a few rounds, then springs into the air where it hangs from a tree branch. It pulls itself up into the tree and scurries into the dying foliage, and disappears.

She stops herself from spraying the tree with bullets. Barely. Because that's what it wants. It wants her to think she has a chance. And when both mags are empty, it'll climb down and twist her up like Captain Bell and his platoon.

This is how these creatures win. They exhaust their prey, then devour.

So, instead of lighting up the tree, she runs away.

It'll follow. She knows it will. If for nothing else, which she doubts, out of curiosity.

Finding Tanner is the main objective, but she can't lead this nasty creature to him. No. She has to kill it somehow. And quickly.

Ghost Rock isn't far from Plains Waterfall. And the waterfall might give her an advantage. Maybe. That's if she can get there and work out a plan before it kills her.

She hears distant, sharp gunshots.

What the hell are they shooting at, anyway?

If there are more teams here, then why aren't they closer? Shouldn't they be? This is where the monster is, after all. But there are more of the original creatures still lurking about. Makes sense. Not *that* many were killed, now that she really thinks about it.

The light fixed to the M4 catches the large, pale monstrosity that's Ghost Rock. She veers to the right of it and sort of stumble walks down the moderate hill. At the bottom, the sound of falling water greets her stronger than ever. The waterfall isn't far now; it's just beyond a stand of blue spruces about fifty yards in front of her.

Kris shines the light around, checking to see if the creature is nearby or watching. All she sees are autumn-shocked trees. Maybe it's watching. Maybe not. Maybe it's eating Captain Bell's men.

The point is right now, she doesn't *feel* it watching her.

Kris draws in a deep breath and blows out a white vapor cloud. Then she runs to the waterfall.

***

A vile animal is what feasts on the dead. Something that's not offspring, but close. Its sole purpose is to feed until full.

It watches this shimmery blue thing and wonders where it came from. The true offspring lies in the discards of its own body, back split wide open. It doesn't take much to piece it all together. Not evolution, this. More like devolution.

The men flood in, but it knows what the creature will do before it moves. It's the slight ticking of instincts. A peculiar signal, a scent that perfumes the air. It's something so faint the men swarming around can't detect it.

They shoot, and in a blink, the beast is gone.

It almost laughs as it watches a bending of light pass in front of tall weeds. Sometimes it's not just speed that confuses, but stealth.

If nothing else, it admires this primitive beast for its defined, though limited, instincts.

It'll make a good guard dog when the time comes, so it lets the thing go for now.

It has more important matters to attend to anyway.

It sneaks away from the men.

***

The mist that rises off the waterfall wets Kris's skin as she ventures closer, deepening the chill.

She surveys the area. Not perfect, but it'll have to do. She's sick of running. Time to make a stand. Plus, the faster she kills the creature, the sooner she can find Tanner and get the hell out of these damn woods.

Not much to work with, though. Two grenades and four shotgun shells, her partial mag in the M4, and the full one in its slot on her belt.

That's it.

With a heavy sigh, Kris gets to work.

She spots a slight part in the trees that gives way to the rocky terrain before the small pond. A natural opening, an easy way in.

It'll work.

She hurries over to it and eyes the length between two of the smaller trees. It's about four feet apart, maybe a little more. Kris pulls the laces out of her boots. She ties a lace to one of the trees while wrapping the other lace around the parallel tree and a grenade. Then she sucks in a breath while she knots the free end of the first lace onto the grenade pin.

Viola. A tripwire. Well, more or less.

What worries her is the four point five second delay. Give or take a second or two, because they're not an exact science. If the creature rushes through, it'll explode behind it, not causing much damage, if at all.

She'll have to shoot at it to keep it close to the grenade.

If not, though, there needs to be a Plan B. There always needs to be a Plan B. Because, more often than not, Plan A's fail or go wonky.

She has one more grenade. But where…?

A series of hollow, dry pops. The sound of snapping sticks.

Kris glances around and hauls ass to one of the larger rocks. Not as big as Ghost Rock, but it'll do. It's large enough to hide behind, at least.

She turns off the light, presses herself up tight against the rock, and waits.

Pale threads of moonlight give the area an ethereal glow, but it's enough to see okay. Not great, but okay. The dark spots, the shadows, they're too deep. Anything might be hiding in them.

She waits.

Another few sticks snap. Her heart thwumps. She absently chews on her bottom lip.

There's a very slim chance the creature will enter through the small opening, but there's still a chance. And that's even if it comes after her.

It didn't seem particularly interested in her. Not like the monster that came out of Brooke. She didn't get the feeling it was solely after her. She doesn't know. All she knows is she need to kill it and find her son.

She listens to the distant single gunshots echo through the woods. The waterfall crashes into the pond.

Kris focuses on the narrow opening with the tripwire. No more sticks snap. Or if they do, she can't hear them over the waterfall.

The smell hits her first. Nothing dead and rotting, but more like cinnamon. A spice smell.

Before she can think, let alone move, a long chittering noise lifts above the crashing water. Her eyes widen when she realizes where the noise is coming from.

Kris lifts her head, slowly. She starts backing away, heart tumbling over itself.

The creature perches on top of the small boulder, following her every movement.

Very slowly, Kris lifts the M4, finger on the trigger—

It leaps off the big rock and slams into her. She lands flat on her back on jagged rocks, the creature on top. She screams as it lunges forward, maw snapping. She manages to get the M4 between them before those teeth bite off her face. It clamps down. Its teeth shriek against metal, squeaks against plastic. It shakes its head back and forth vigorously, like a dog with a chew toy. The creature is so strong she almost loses her grip on the gun. Still, she holds on. She has to. The M4 is the only thing saving her ass right now.

One of its slender claws rakes across her chest, ripping through her jacket and slicing skin. The pain is like being stabbed with a branding iron. Kris roars into the creature's face, pushing it away as it lunges and shakes, trying to rid her of the M4. Tentacles begin to slowly wrap around her torso, working on squeezing and neutralizing her.

With it chomping on the M4, she has no other weapon. None, except…

The last grenade shifts heavily in her jacket pocket. All well and good, but how the hell is she supposed to pull the pin one handed? Going all Action Star and using her teeth to pull the pin will no doubt result in a few loose teeth, or worse. Probably worse. Grenade pins aren't *that* easy to pull. They are designed specifically not to pull easily to avoid accidents.

Still, she lets go of the M4 with her left hand, right arm trembling as the thing shakes and presses down. The gun tilts toward her face. Kris reaches into her jacket pocket.

Hot drool gloops onto her chest. The thing's breath has a cloying sweet smell she can't place. The tentacles squeeze.

Kris brings the grenade up, clamps onto the pin with her mouth, and says good-bye to her teeth as she yanks.

There's a harsh ripping sound in her head. Pain surges to her sinuses, coils around her ears, rages in her temples. Blood floods her mouth, a deep coppery taste.

But the pin comes out with an audible clink.

The creature lunges a final time and she shoves the grenade into its mouth. She watches it recoil, then swallows it down. Then she's thrashing to get the thing off of her. When the grenade explodes, she'll get nailed, too. It clamps back down on the M4.

Kris knees it in the stomach, but the tentacles remain fixed. She pushed back on the M4 and the monster pushes forward. Her shoulders burn from the strain, arms trembling. Blood seeps, wetting both shoulders from the punctures and the fresher claw marks.

How long has it been? Three seconds? Four?

She flails, twisting this way and that. The tentacles loosen a bit, but not much. It's enough to wiggle her legs up a little as she pushes the thing back, back—

Her world becomes a splash of gore and agony when the creature's stomach explodes. It sways, releases a long groan, and plops down on top of her. It doesn't move. Its weight is crushing. Her right leg screams. Dark blood coats her body. It's hot, slippery, and absolutely foul. Human sewage is the closest comparison.

Kris rolls the creature off of her and screams. She can't help it. It feels like hundreds of dull knives twisting in her leg.

Scooting away, dragging the M4 along, her screams dull to thick grunt in her throat. Kris looks at her right leg. In the pale glow of the moon, she can't tell what's her blood and the creatures. It's all colorless and dark.

She pulls the M4 closer, turns on the LED, and points it at her leg.

For a moment, she can't breathe. Can't even acknowledge what she's seeing.

The beast's blood, it's not black like the other. It's a strange bronze color. The blood doesn't move, either, thank God. Through the bronze blood is her own, red and terrifying. It confirms that she's hurt. Maybe horribly. Maybe the shock has taken away most of the pain.

If anything wants to kill her, now is the perfect time. She's pretty much helpless.

She strips off her jacket and wipes away as much of the gross bronze blood as she can. Then, using the light, she inspects the wound closer. In a way, she wishes she hadn't.

Wounds, though. Not wound.

There are seven holes in her jeans. Protruding from each is a shiny, blood-tinged shard of shrapnel.

She's never gotten hit by a grenade before, but from having to deal with taking care of a few soldiers over the years, she knows getting the shrapnel out as soon as possible is a must. Or, wait, is it she's supposed to leave the metal in because of blood loss and infection?

With the thing's blood mingling with hers, infection is pretty much a guarantee.

Kris grips a piece of shrapnel near her knees and pulls. The pain is a bolt of lightning up her leg. She cries out. Her vision blurs and stomach quivers. Everything inside contracts. The world around her becomes an unsubstantial thing, wavering.

Finally, the pain ebbs and everything eases a bit. She wipes tears away and looks around. The dark mound of the creature lies no more than four or five feet away. She stares at it for a long time, then looks away.

Kris is about to attempt to stand when a voice rises slightly above the waterfall.

"Mom? Mom, where are you?"

"Tanner," she whispers and finishes gaining her feet.

The pain is intense, but her son is out there. Her baby needs her. A growl rumbles in her throat as she powers forward, putting as much weight on her left leg as possible. She limps in the direction of Tanner's voice.

"Mom? Help. I'm scared!"

"I-I'm coming, honey. Just…just stay there."

She limps a few more feet. "Keep talking and don't move."

Faint, but there, "Okay, Mom."

Kris stops at the narrow opening, stares at the tripwire. She about steps over it, but changes her mind. What if someone trips it?

"Mom, Mel left me. Please hurry!"

A small whine escapes her throat. She kneels, carefully, and unties the trap. She drops the grenade into her jacket pocket. She pockets the laces as well. There is no time to weave them back into her boots. Using the small trees for support, Kris pulls herself back onto her feet. For a minute or so, she doesn't move. She shuts her eyes, drawing in deep breaths, as pain stabs through her right leg.

"Mom?"

Her eyes pop open. Gritting her teeth, she limps forward.

"I'm here," she shouts. "Just keep talking!"

But as she tries to move forward, the pain freezes her. She about collapses, and might have if not for a low-hanging branch.

Kris looks around. *I need a crutch.*

Faint, more so than before, “Hurry, Mom!”

No time for finding a makeshift crutch. Tanner is moving. Maybe something is after him?

“Hold on, honey,” she shouts. “I’m on my way!”

Not as distant, she hears the occasional gunshots. Someone shouts something but she can’t quite make it out.

Teeth clenched, Kris limps deeper into the woods, shouting for her son.

***

They struggle against the stuff holding them to the trees. White vapor puffs out of their nostrils. Their mouths are sealed by the gauzy substance keeping them prisoner.

It grins, savoring their terror, feeding off it.

A part of it doesn’t want to do this, but only a small part. A sliver, really. A distant babble, much like the shouting woman out there.

It turns away from its prey and ventures back into the woods for more.

***

M4 in one hand, but too heavy to keep up for much longer than a couple minutes at a time to use the light, Kris calls out to Tanner.

Again, he doesn’t answer.

Something must be chasing him or he’s hiding and trying to be quiet for now, waiting for whatever it is to leave. Either/or, it’s pissing her off. They need to go attack the soldiers and leave her son alone.

The fiery agony of her right leg slows her down considerably.

The things one does in a desperate situation. She’s seen it happen with even her own team. One of hers, Sara Reynolds, got trapped under a car, and out of her mind with pain, this soldier chose to bury a grenade near her under the wreckage. Probably to create a crater for her to fall into and crawl out from the wreckage, Kris assumed. The woman wouldn't want to be rescued.

This soldier, Kris's soldier, didn't bury the grenade nearly deep enough, and when it went off, it took her and most of her head with it.

At the time, Kris hadn't understood why she decided to do what she did. What could possibly drive someone to go as far as to risk their own life like that?

Now, Kris gets it. Terror and pain breeds desperation.

If she hadn't used the grenade on the creature, she'd be dead now, a twisted corpse like Captain Bell and his platoon.

A life or death situation.

Kris lifts the M4 and shines the light around. The woods feel too empty now. It's too quiet, save for the random gunshots in the distance. Like the place is holding its breath, like it's suffocating.

She needs Tanner to call to her again. Needs a direction.

"Tanner," she shouts, voice ping-ponging off the trees.

No answer.

Kris limps onward, calling out her son's name between surges of agony laddering up her leg to her hip.

Then…

"Mom! Over here!" On her right a bit. Not too far.

Her heart quickens, stomach contracting. She turns right and pushes herself toward his voice.

"I'm over here! Mom, help!"

Sobs catch in her throat. Tears spill down her cheeks.

She stumbles out of the woods and onto the dirt road. She can see the Explorer from here.

"Hurry, Mom! It's…"

Silence.

"N-no."

Kris hurries as fast as she can down the road.

***

Berk rubs the space between his eyes and sighs. "When was their last check-in?"

Private Silva, in Berk's office, says, "2300, or so, sir."

Berk nods. “Not long then.” Right now, in civilian time, it’s a couple minutes after midnight. Not long? It’s been over an hour. Still, the teams have a lot on their plates right now.

“Sir?”

Berk blinks, returns his attention to Silva. “Yes?”

“Our last communication was from an unknown source in the SEALs team. He said all targets have been eliminated and they were going to locate the survivors.”

Berk frowns. “You point, Private? I don’t see how—”

“Exactly two minutes before that, sir, Captain Bell reported they were experiencing severe casualties before the coms went down.”

For a moment, either from lack sleep or old age creeping up on him, Berk just stares at Private Silva, not connecting the dots. Then, slowly, his eyes widen. His rises out of his chair.

“Oh, God.” He barely recognizes his own voice.

32

Sobbing, Kris limps toward the Explorer. Her leg burns, and every time she accidently put pressure on it, it's an inferno of agony that drives all reason out of her mind for a few minutes.

She goes to the driver's side window and peers in. The SUV is empty. Wiping tears from her cheeks, Kris backs away in an awkward hop. Her heel kicks something and she hears a clinking noise. She shines the light at the ground.

Metal glitters at her.

Carefully, she bends and picks up her keys, the ones she gave to Mel. She holds them up to the light, all the air in her lungs seeping out.

They didn't make it.

"No," she croaks, good leg quivering. She balances herself against the Explorer's hood, her body a mess of twitches and shivers.

She swipes damp strands of hair away from her face.

"No," she repeats. "No." She slams a fist down on the hood. "No!" She slams her fist down again. Harder. "Nonononono." She pummels the hood with all of her rage, all of her sorrow and pain. Over and over she beats on the hood of her vehicle, leaving shallow dents behind.

Should've went with them. Should've protected them. Why do I always have to be so stupid? Why—?

"Mom?" The voice comes from up the road, back toward the woods.

Kris sucks in a sharp breath, stumbles away from the Explorer. She limps a few yards up the road. "T-Tanner?"

"Mom, help." On her three, beyond the edge of the woods, she hears a quick crackling swishing sound, like someone running through dead leaves.

Kris points the light at the woods. "Tanner? Where are you?"

On her left, she hears a whisper. "Here."

She whirls, but all her light finds are more trees, thick bushes, and tangles of dying weeds.

A strange smell swirls around her. Cloying. It's a scent of strange sweetness, with ominous intentions.

Something crashes through the woods, once more too hidden by the woods to see.

"What now?" Kris asks the night, tracking the noisy progress until it stops and silence once more envelopes her.

There's another monster. She can almost feel it. The fear plucks at her nerve endings. Another one, but how is she going to stay upright while shooting the M4? The recoil isn't massive, but she hurts so much all over, she's not even sure she can lift the thing for long.

The Explorer.

Yes.

She can get in, prop the gun on the door, and shoot.

Kris turns to the SUV, limps forward.

From an overhanging branch, a man drops onto the hood of her vehicle, caving it in severely. *Crump.*

Kris stops and lifts the M4, about to shoot. Already her arms tremble with the weight.

The man, dressed in all black tactical gear, holds his hands up in a show of surrender, showing Kris he means no harm.

She doesn't lower the gun, however. No matter how much her arms shake and cry to her brain, no matter the hot, miserable agony coursing up her leg, she keeps the muzzle pointing at him.

His bald head gleams in the glare of the LED. His eyes are calm, squinty from the light. His calm, almost arrogant demeanor cries SEAL to her. Just in the way he stands, she can tell he's a part of one of the best branches in the military.

"Hi," he says, voice very deep. "I'm Chief Haims of the US Navy SEALs, here to exterminate the threat and escort you to safety." He lifts a dark eyebrow. "I assume you're one of the survivors?"

"Where are the others?" Kris asks, trying to control the pain from leaking into her voice. Standing like this cuts into her nerve. She fights screaming. The leg is the worst.

"We're locating the other survivors, ma'am."

She blinks. “Other survivors? They find them yet?”

He nods. “Missing one. The woman with the kids said there’s a boy out there named Tanner. We’re searching for him.”

“T-Tanner? He’s my son!”

Chief Haims smiles a bit. “I’m sure we’ll find him.” He lowers his hands. “The way you hold that M4, it’s like you’ve had practice.”

Kris sighs. “Sergeant Jenner, US Army Special Ops.”

Haims nods. “We weren’t briefed on backgrounds. Good to know you’re part of the team.” He frowns. “How injured are you?”

Kris lowers the gun so it’s out of Haim’s eyes. “Shrapnel in the right leg. Puncture wounds in shoulders. Lots of cuts and bruises.”

“Holy shit,” Haims says and jumps off the hood to the ground gracefully, like he’s jumped off many hoods in his lifetime. He starts toward her but then stops. “I’m just coming over to check your wounds. We have a medic on hand.”

Kris shrugs. “Okay. Sorry. Been a helluva night.” She cringes at the sound of her own craggy voice.

“I know,” Haims says, moving closer. “But it’s over now. They’re all dead. Good thing you killed that monster at the waterfall. Might’ve snuck right by us.”

A frown swarms over Kris’s face. “How’d you know that?”

Haims pause. “Know what?”

Hand gripping the M4 tighter, Kris hops back a few steps. “How’d you know I killed it? And where?”

Haims shrugs. “I stumbled across the body and connected the dots.”

“Then you should’ve seen my light. Not like I’m Speed Racer here.” Kris gently pats her right leg.

Haims shakes his head. “Didn’t see you. Must’ve taken a different route.”

Kris lifts the M4, light full force in his face. “How’d you know I was here, then?”

Haims looks away, and when his face returns to the light, a leering grin cuts across his face. “I followed my nose.” His voice is different. Thicker. More like he's growling at her than talking now.

He moves closer. Stops. His long grin barely falters as he says, "Your species is no longer top of the food chain." The grin lengthens and keeps lengthening until Haims's cheeks split open. Blood pours down his neck. Stings of flesh barely connect between the lower jaw and cheeks. Thin, black tendrils wriggle through holes and tears in the skin.

Kris pulls the trigger, sending rapid bursts of lead into Haims's chest. He jitters with the impacts and drops to his knees.

She doesn't hesitate and pulls the last grenade from her jacket pocket, ending this before shit gets worse, as it has been all night.

Kris yanks the pin out, about to throw it, when Haims, or whatever he is now, says, "Help me, Mom! Help," in Tanner's voice. Haims stands. "I'm so scared, Mom! Please help!" A gurgly chuckle vomits out of Haims's wide gash of a mouth.

The son of a bitch.

Kris throws the grenade at the creature. It leaps away. The grenade clunks onto the hood of the Explorer. She has less than a second to realize this before she drops to the ground and the front end of her vehicle is obliterated, quaking the world. Things whiz by her, over her. Jagged chunks of her SUV sprinkle the ground. Something hot bounces of the small of her back, and she's sure she'll have a nice big bruise there.

Once the raining pieces of her SUV stop, Kris uses the M4 to regain her feet. The leg is a pillar of agony.

The entire front end of the Explorer is engulfed in flames.

The sweet, high laughter of a child echoes through the woods. Then, Tanner's voice says, "I bet you can't find me, Mom."

"Why are you doing this?" Kris shouts.

"Because I *love* you, Mom."

"Leave us alone!"

"But we're having so much fun!"

"*Where's my son*?"

"Dead." That last response came from the left side of the road, just far enough away to echo back into the woods

A deep ache squeezes her heart. No. It can't be true.

It wants her to follow it. But why? Why not just kill her now? If Tanner is really dead, then she has nothing left to live for anyway.

Something like an epiphany hits her. Before her mind's eye, she sees this thing leaving the woods. She sees it breeding, or whatever it does. Spreading. Eventually, it'll take over the world and start the slow death of humanity.

Much as she had with the other things. Only worse.

And if Tanner is dead…

Kris limps toward the edge of the road and stares into the dark woods. The outer corner of her left eye ticks. She draws in a deep breath, and releases the loudest roar she can manage. A raw, savage sound; rage that burns her throat like straight whiskey.

The pain in her leg is an afterthought as she crashes into the woods after the monster.

***

The woman's roar fades, and for the first time since it came to consciousness, it felt a sliver of fear.

It sprints through the woods toward the other woman and the children, knowing the men heard Sergeant Jensen, knowing they no doubt heard the grenade explode, too. They'll be heading this way. It can take out Sergeant Jensen no problem, should've back there, but if the men find it…

No time to think about that right now.

It has much to do before leaving the woods.

So much…

***

Anger rages through her as she works her way back into the woods. Her teeth grit the pain in her leg away. She doesn't have time for it.

"Come back here, you piece of shit," she shouts, voice cracking on the last word. "Damn coward! Get back here and face me!"

Of course, there's no answer. No sounds at all. As it has been all night, save for the shooting and screaming, Maker's Woods is silent. Where are the rest of the SEALs? There has to be more. Unless it killed them, too, and she's alone with it in these woods. If so, she's the last hope at stopping it before it escapes, if that's what it wants to do. Maybe it doesn't. Maybe it wants to toy with her awhile, then kill her. She doesn't know. The thing is, she needs to find it and kill it. That's her mission. That's her objective. Find. Kill. For Tanner. Screw everyone else. Her entire family is gone.

A growl rumbles in her throat. She swipes the M4 back and forth, cutting the darkness like a sharp blade through paper with the LED light.

"Where are you?"

Only the quiet, dark night replies.

She sweeps the light back and forth, up and down as she limps through skiffs of dead leaves and brush. But the creature is gone. Just—

"Freeze! US Marines!"

Kris stops so suddenly she falls forward, catches herself on a branch, and manages to land on her knees. She screams as the pain in her leg cuts through her rage.

Four men circle her, guns aimed and ready.

"I-I'm Sergeant Jensen of the US Army Special Ops. Platoon code name, Viper."

They don't move or say anything for a full minute or so.

Then one of the men says, "Lower 'em. Help her up."

They do as their leader orders them to and help her to her feet. She cries out again from the burning in her right leg.

With their guns lowered, the light around the area is dim. The leader of the group says, "Ma'am, what happened to your leg?"

"Grenade."

He nods and says, "Medic."

A very tall man crouches down in front of her, flashlight in hand, as he inspects her leg. After a moment, he whistles.

"What?" Kris manages, trying to power through the agony.

"Sir," the medic says, not speaking to her. "She has seven shards in her leg. Pretty banged up. Probably severely infected, judging by the discoloration of the skin."

The leader sighs. He glances around. Then to the other two says, "Keep watch."

They nod and take up spots in front and behind Kris.

"Ma'am," the medic says. "I'm going to need you to sit down, if you can."

Something crashes through the brush on their right. A child's laughter rises in the chilly air.

"Medic," the leader says. "Hold off on that. We have company."

The medic tells Kris to just be still and grabs his gun. They form four points around her, each taking a side. Kris picks up her own gun; screw what the medic said, she needs to be on her feet. She needs to fight. Revenge is all that's on her mind now. It found her instead of her finding it, but oh well. Now she can kill it.

She stands, growling against all the pain, and says, "Hit it hard and don't stop firing until it's dead." She sweeps sparse leaves off the canopy with her light. "It'll try to trick you. Make you think it's somewhere else when it's not. Don't fire until you actually see it."

None of the men say anything, nor acknowledge her, but she knows they heard her. She just hopes they do what she says.

"Mom…Mommy…heeelp…"

The very sound of Tanner's voice sends wave after wave of chills through her.

"Heeelp meee, Mommy."

A few dead leaves see-saw to the ground in front of her. She points the light up, scanning the trees. But if it's up there, she can't see it. And if it's still in Haims's body, or whatever is going on, then she should be able to see it fairly well. There's nothing, though. Just branches of dying leaves.

High-pitched giggling fills the night.

"It's in the body of a SEAL," Kris blurts. "Don't look for a monster. Look for—"

The medic drops a second before she hears the gunshot.

The other three Marines clustered closer to her, sweeping their gun lights.

The leader says, “Steady.”

A long silence, then, “Come on, Mommy. Let’s play.”

Another gunshot. The soldier on her right cries out and falls to his knees. He’s clutching his shoulder.

“Oops,” the thing says in Tanner’s voice.

Crack!

Blood mists the air in front of Kris and the soldier falls face first into leaves.

“Two more to go, Mommy.”

Kris grabs the leader’s arm. He looks at her with wide, pissed-off eyes.

“It wants me,” she says. “It’ll keep doing this until I go out there.”

He doesn’t say anything for a while. He pulls out of her grip, watches the woods. In a voice almost too low to hear, he says, “No. We were sent here to eliminate the threat. To protect and rescue. You’re not going anywhere.”

“But it’ll shoot you both, then come after me anyway.”

He shrugs. “Then so be it. But I think we can take it, right, Flynn?”

The other remaining Marine whispers, “Hoo-Rah.”

Two seconds later, most of his brains are splattered all over the back of the leader.

Frantic, heart trying to claw out of her chest, she turns the leader to her. “Look, you don’t need to die. You can run. Get more help. I’ll try to hold it here.”

He shakes his head slowly. “Just use that M4 when I tell you.”

Kris grits her teeth, limps around, and is face to face with Haims’s tattered, bloody grin.

“Hello, Mommy,” it says. Thin tentacles squirm out of holes like lethargic snakes. Slow. Sleepy. Its eyes are completely black, like two polished onyx stones.

It shoves her aside before she can shoot it. Kris lands on top of the dead medic. She scrambles off, pain clamping onto her right leg.

The leader of the Marine team buries his knife into the creature's throat. He boots it in the stomach, pushing it away from Kris. The thing controlling Haims gurgles and coughs, hand on the knife's handle.

The Marine leader slams the muzzle of his pistol against the creature's waxy forehead, and blows a hole through its head. It sways for a few seconds, then crumbles to the ground. The sluggish tentacles fall limp.

Breathing heavily, the Marine turns to Kris as she struggles to stand. He helps steady her and says, "That's how a Marine handles a situation."

Kris's sight jitters to the dead creature, waiting for it to move, waiting for it to spring back up and rip a hole through the Marine leader. But it doesn't. It remains flat on its back, knife still stuck in its throat.

"I'm Captain Rogers, by the way," he says and spares a glance at his fallen team. "They were great soldiers. Last of the team I brought here."

"I'm sorry," Kris says. All of the madness she's been through tonight is tearing her down. Everything feels too heavy. Her body is a constant, throbbing ache.

Rogers nods. "Yeah." He gently pulls her right arm over his broad shoulders. "Let's get you out of here."

She doesn't protest. There's no reason to be in Maker's Woods. Not now. Tears well in her head. Tanner. Her baby. He's gone. Just like Kyle, taken from her. Ripped out of her like a vital organ. A sob catches in her throat.

"You're going to be okay, Sergeant," Rogers says, trying to be soothing, and failing. He's much too amped up by everything, too stuck in the battle mindset yet. It happens.

"My son," she manages. "It killed him."

Rogers nods once, lips pressing together in a thin, tight line on his face. He doesn't say anything, but she can tell it struck something in him. Maybe he has a son, too? Soldiers are humans, too. Sometimes people forget that. Hell, even the soldiers themselves forget from time to time. Sometimes they just get locked into the mechanics of things. So much so, they begin acting like a machine themselves.

Kris is so wrapped up in her thoughts, her sorrow, that she barely hears the hissing behind them. And when it does register, it's already too late.

Something slams into Rogers's back, driving him face first into the ground. Kris flails, her support gone. She catches her balance, resting all her weight on the leg, and lifts the assault rifle.

Perched on top of Rogers—like an obscene gargoyle—the thing that used to be Haims throws back its head and howls a long, trembling shriek. It yanks the knife out of its neck. The black tentacles slither up the top half of its head. Wet crackling sounds pollute Kris's hearing. Underneath, Rogers writhed. Every time he tries to get up, the creature slams him back down.

The wet crackling sounds worsen. And before she can work herself up to shoot the thing, Haims's entire head splits open from the jaw joint up. Its lower jaw dangles on red sinews as the rest of the head splits, black tentacles doing all the work.

"Jesus," Kris croaks, eyes wide.

She watches its skull collapse like a convertible. Her gorge rises and she fights the sudden urge to vomit... Not that there's anything left in her stomach anyway.

The top half of the human head plops on to the back of Rogers's legs, and from out of the opening, something cocooned in a thin, gray membrane emerges. The tentacles whip and snap, no longer the sluggish things they were before. They lash around the membranous thing protruding out of the neck as it stretches further.

Barely breathing, Kris can't find the strength to pull the trigger. She can hardly hold the M4 up.

Rogers roars something, but his face is too buried in a pile of dead leaves to understand what he's saying, if he's saying anything at all. Not that she can do a damn thing right now. Watching the thing tear out of Brooke had been the worst, but this...somehow it's worse. More menacing. Like Haims is growing a new...

"Head," she whispers as wave after wave of the chills spill through her.

The thing pulling out of Haims's neck is another head.

This revelation spurs her stomach into a sickening lurch. Her body so desperately wants to vomit, but she wills the feeling away. She can't do that. It'll distract her too long. She needs to do something. And soon, before it…

The tentacles strip away the thin, gray membrane as the new head fully adjusts itself. Brackish liquid splashes the still-human shoulders. The new head makes squelching noises as it stretches its jaw. The only comparison Kris can think of that fits is that the head resembles a dragon, albeit a deformed one. V-shaped, but not quite. Its skin appears slimy, and jet black.

Then it opens its maw wide, expelling a shrill scream. Long, pointy teeth glimmer in the glow of the gun's light.

Long, ashen talons slice out of the tips of Haims's fingers. They dig into Rogers's back. His screams are muffled, choked with leaves.

Kris tries making her finger pull the trigger, but it refuses to listen. Her body is like a numb, dead thing. A statue frozen in place, forced to bear witness to this horror show.

The claws pull down Rogers's back, raking deep furrows. Rogers's kicks his legs, screaming. He's trying to roll over, and that's when she notices why he hasn't rolled the thing off of him since it perched there.

Another tentacle coming out of Haims's side wraps around the captain's waist. It's holding him in place; it has been since it pounced.

Images of Tanner shuffle through her mind. Baby Tanner in her arms not long after his birth. Tanner on his sixth birthday unwrapping his presents, jumping up and down with joy when Kyle brought out his very own bow and arrow set. Tanner smiling and laughing. Tanner crawling into bed with her and Kyle during thunderstorms at night. Tanner giving her random kisses on the cheek. Tanner…

Kris blinks and the images fade. Replacing it is the old rage she felt earlier, the mad rage; the kind where all that matters is killing the thing that took her baby.

Kris pulls the M4's trigger.

***

It's transforming. An unexpected change, but a welcome one all the same. It's becoming its own species, as it knew it has been all along.

For a moment, it's in pure ecstasy. Here it is, being born, a new thing in the world. It has so much to do. Sudden needs cumulate within. Where once all it wanted to do is toy with the woman and spread its seed, now it wants to run. It wants to leave the woods and create its own place in this world. It—

Then pain rips through it every part of it. It cries out, twists its head, and sees the source of the agony.

The woman. It vaguely remembers her. The host's brain knew her better. To it, she didn't matter much, really. All it saw was food. Prey. Something to play with before devouring.

Whatever she's doing, she's creating the pain.

It leaps at her.

***

One thing she realizes shortly after pumping it with a few rounds is the thing doesn't heal itself like the one that came out of Brooke. Its yellow blood flows, pooling onto Rogers.

She notes this a second or two before it shrieks and leaps at her.

She puts some weight on the pillar of agony that's her leg to steady herself, and lifts the gun. Bullets plunge into its freshly born head, shearing off the entire left side. Yellow blood sprays.

Then it crashes into her.

There's a sharp pain in the back of her head.

Darkness follows.

33

Slowly, like thick morning fog, the darkness slips away. Kris opens her eyes to slits and shuts them again. Her head is a turmoil of crushing pains. Eventually, the incredible ache reduces, focusing on a spot on the back of her head.

As the ache locks itself in one place for now, she's aware of a great weight on top of her. Making it hard to breathe.

Kris opens her eyes again, this time keeping them open. She sucks in a sharp breath. Long, sharp teeth lie on her chest, inches from her face. It takes her a while to realize the thing on top of her isn't moving. Yellow blood soaks through her jacket and shirt. It's still warm.

She thrashes, frantically shoving the body off of her and pulling herself away from it, grabbing her gun as she does. She quickly sees what knocked her out. A knobby rock about the size of softball sticks out of the ground. There's a bit of blood on it.

The thing remains still. Its face is a mass of yellow, which looks a little like the insides of a pumpkin.

"You…okay?"

She looks up. Swaying over her is Captain Rogers. His eyelids flutter, eyeballs rolling. He looks like he's on the verge of passing out.

"I—yeah," she says and points her gun at the body. "Is it dead?"

Rogers turns to the body, looks at it for a moment, then faces her again. "Better be."

"It clawed your back up," she says. "Can you walk?"

Rogers doesn't answer her. Instead, he stumbles away.

"Hey," she says. "Where you going?"

He continues into the woods.

"Captain?"

After a while, she no longer hears his shuffling progress through the leaves and weeds. She's alone. In front of her is the dead thing. Or at least she hopes it's dead. If this was a horror movie, it'd be the part where the killer makes a surprise attack, or lunge, or something.

She waits, even nudges it with the muzzle of the M4. Nothing.

Kris stands and limps closer to the thing, presses the muzzle to its decimated head, and fires a round into its skull. The entire body jerks, but that's all.

She spits on it, turns, and limps away.

And if it's still alive. If it still wants to kill her. Well…then so be it.

***

She intends on finding the road again and making her way to town, but instead finds herself at Ghost Rock.

The loss swells once more, though no tears form. Perhaps she's cried all that she can for now. Dehydration? Maybe. Close enough.

"Look after my boy," she says to the skeleton wrapped around the base of the boulder. "I don't know why you're here, or how you died, but please, watch over him. He's a good boy. And if you can hear me…tell him I love him."

She moves away and makes her way toward the road.

Not long after, she limps through a thicket and on the other side…

Kris stops, the gun's light shaking with her body. Her mouth opens, closes, opens. And when she catches her breath, she manages, "T-Tanner?"

She moves the light from one wide-eyed face to the other. Mel, Avery, Tanner, Mark, Back to Tanner.

They're plastered to trees with the very same stuff Avery had been, the sticky, cob-webby substance. They struggle against it, but it's too strong. How long have they been here, though? And how many times did she pass right by them? These very questions form a slick ball in the pit of her stomach.

Kris, a whine forming in her throat, limps to them.

Using Mel's knife, she cuts away the sticky substance away from Tanner and pulls him to her. His embrace is shaky. His mind and body have been through so much. His breathing in her ear is nothing but gasps and groans.

Eventually, she talks him into letting go so she can free the others.

She doesn't want to leave him, though. Not after the hellish night they survived… Barely survived. So she has him stand close while she cuts Mel, Mark, and Avery free.

Mel gives her a long hug. When they part, the woman says, "They all dead?"

Kris nods, though she can't be sure. What if one of the original creatures managed to sneak out of the woods? It's possible. If so…not good.

"Oh damn," Mel says, eyeing Kris's leg. "You need a doctor. Like two hours ago."

"Yeah," Kris says. "Grenade. Long story."

Mel smiles the tiniest bit and lets Kris use her as support.

"Let's get the hell out of these woods," Kris croaks. "Nature is *highly* overrated."

They all manage to laugh at this, even the kids. Weak, tired laughter. But laughter all the same. It feels good.

With Kris using Mel as a sort of crutch, they make their way to the dirt road.

The Explorer is still smoldering.

"What the hell?" Mel ventures.

"Eh…" Kris shrugs. "Another grenade."

Mel looks from her to the SUV. She doesn't say anything more, just nods.

They continue down the road, Kris clasping Tanner's hand in her own, never wanting to let go.

Through the opening in the trees above, the first mellow glow of dawn finds Kris's face, soothing the chill of night on her bruised skin.

By the time they reach the end of the dirt road, morning arrives in all its bright splendor. Birds sing and life returns; life waking up after a night no one will ever forget, a night that will haunt her forever.

For now, though, Kris smiles as the sun washes over her. It's over. She has to keep reminding herself of this. It's over. Finally, the night, the darkness…it's over.

SOMEWHERE IN EASTERN IOWA

General Berk watches them exit Maker's Woods on the satellite thermal cam, and blows out a long breath of relief.

All threats have been eliminated. At the cost of many men's live, though. And it's this fact which wells so much deep sorrow within him. No one should've died last night. The threats should've been easy to handle. It just proves they aren't ready for an interdimensional attack, if it happens again.

Well, he plans on changing that with specialized training for his troops, along with building four special operations platoons trained specifically to deal with such threats.

To Private Silva, he says, "Have a pick-up meet them and take them home, Silva." He watches as they turn onto the main road toward Maker's Town. "We're in Sergeant Jensen's debt. See that they're well treated and all medical expenses taken care of."

"Yes, sir." Silva snaps a salute and hurries out of Berk's office. The cleanup crew is en route to dispose of all the remains and collect the fallen soldiers. The creatures' remains are to be shipped to NASA, but he can't do that. They should have all that they need. He's already given the orders to incinerate the remains and destroy any evidence.

He doesn't know all that they do, but can almost see them meddling with stuff they shouldn't be. That's how bad things happen. Like the breach at Area 0. The real Area 51. Something almost got out of that facility. And if it had…well, humans would be fighting to survive right now.

He's just about to close out of the thermal cam when something catches his eyes. He draws in a slow breath, zooming in on the image.

His eyes widen.

Inside one of the survivors is a bright red spot… A spot none of the others have.

Berk's breath wheezes out.

The spot, it's inside one of the kids.

The one holding who he assumes is Sergeant Jensen's hand.

For a long time, Berk doesn't breathe. He doesn't move.

His hand trembles as he reaches for the phone.

THE END

www.ingramcontent.com/pod-product-compliance
Lightning Source LLC
Chambersburg PA
CBHW072238190626
46809CB00018B/2849

* 9 7 8 1 9 2 5 5 9 7 1 6 5 *